ARTFUL EVIL

C.G. HARRIS

Hot
Chocolate
Press

The Judas Files *a 5-book action-packed, supernatural series filled with snarky characters & dark humor.*

The Judas Files Completed Series:

Book 1-THE NINE

Book 2-NEW DOMINION

Book 3-ARTFUL EVIL

Book 4 - WAR ORIGIN

Book 5 - FINAL RUIN

<u>Download the FREE SHORT STORY,</u> Exiled

Join the C.G. Harris Legion
Join the C.G. Harris Legion to receive book intel, useless trivia, special giveaways, plus you'll learn about Hula Harry and get his Drink of the Week.
https://www.cgharris.net/legion-sign-up-page

Printed in the United States of America: First Printing, 2021
Hot Chocolate Press, Fort Collins, Colorado
Cover design by: Karri Klawiter
Print ISBN: 978-1733334198

WWW.CGHARRIS.NET

CHAPTER ONE

F ights in The Nine usually ended up in one of two ways; either you won, or you were dead—again—and found yourself in the Gnashing Fields. The winner wasn't so much the problem. The dead guy, he was bad for business. Not my business, of course. I worked for The Judas Agency, A.K.A. The Disaster Factory. They thrived on death, dismemberment, and destruction. My friend, Dan, was a different story. He was a conservative guy straight out of the 60's. He owned Hula Harry's. One of the only torture free establishments in Hell. I wasn't about to let a couple of beefeaters bust up his joint with their brawl. I laced my fingers into my Knuckle Stunner and pulled it out of my pocket. There was no need for subterfuge. By the time either of them registered my involvement in their little sideshow, the first guy was flat on the ground.

The Knuckle Stunner was a Hellion-made weapon that somehow scrambled the circuits in the brain. The harder you hit someone, the thicker the scramble. I had set the first guy on purée and was headed for the second when he put his hands up in surrender.

"Sorry, man. He wouldn't stop bugging me! What was I supposed to do?"

"First, you're in a bar where you can't get drunk." It was true. Booze didn't work in The Nine because, well ... Hell. "You have no excuse for acting like a stupid frat boy. Second, grab your new buddy and drag him out of here. You're both banned for two weeks."

"What? That's not fa—"

I cut him off by raising my Knuckle Stunner in his direction. "If I have to drag you both out, it's six weeks, and you don't want me to pick the drop spot. I know a lot of back alley cesspools with your name on them."

Frat Boy didn't say another word. He just nodded, bent over, and dragged his penance toward the door.

"Any of you good citizens willing to help this young man out?" I looked around the bar. Everyone seemed unusually preoccupied with their tabletops.

"A free drink for anyone who helps him." Dan wandered in behind me. The yellow button-down he wore was so thin you could almost read the tag on his undershirt, but somehow, he made it work.

The bar came to life with the sound of scraping chairs and shuffling feet. I half expected another fight to break out over who got to help him. Hard to believe a free drink full of impotent booze could be so effective.

"Thanks for your help, Gabe—again." Dan smoothed out his thinning hair and turned to look at me. "You do so much around here I feel like you should be a partner."

I shoved the Knuckle Stunner back into my pocket and turned away from the gaggle of makeshift rescue workers. "No, thanks. I have enough irons stoking in the fire. I can't keep them all hot as it is."

Dan laughed. "Still, I owe you for everything you have done for me around here."

"You owe me nothing. Spending time here is a pleasure. Besides, where else can I hide out from all my responsibilities?" I put a hand on Dan's shoulder. "Speaking of hiding, I finished my little project in the back room. Why don't you come take a look?"

Hula Harry's was an unusual place for many reasons. Yes, it was a torture-free establishment. That in and of itself made the place an oddity in The Nine. Most establishments thrived on some sort of violence or cruelty as a form of entertainment, all fully endorsed by Hell's management, of course. Hula Harry's was different. It was just a local bar filled with Woebegone souls looking to pass eternity any way they could, even if they couldn't catch a buzz.

The original Harry, whoever he was, had built the place entirely out of crushed cars. The walls were bricked with cube shaped monstrosities of rims, axles, and Detroit steel. The multi-colored marvel was a sight to behold. It also made Hula Harry's one of the most solid structures in the area.

We strolled past the bar, made from old school bus doors, and headed into the back. "Your storeroom's as safe as a titanium piggy bank. No one will lay a hand on your precious inventory now."

Dan peered around the seemingly empty room, seeing nothing but a few shelves— that, and the false wall I had installed to hide his valuable stock.

"That's incredible, Gabe." He lowered his voice so the nearby patrons wouldn't overhear. "What's the secret to getting in?"

I motioned him away from any prying eyes, then I reached down and hit the hidden catch in the wall. The door swung away and revealed Dan's treasure trove of black-market goods. Case after case of sugar-loaded soda. We didn't waste time with the diet stuff. We were in Hell after all.

"Fantastic." Dan clapped me on the shoulder. "Keep this up, and I'll have to hire you on full-time for sure."

I laughed. "I wish. Working here would be a lot more fun than my regular gig."

"I don't know how I'm going to pay you back for all of this."

I shrugged. "This was nothing. I've learned a trick or two along the way. Sometimes you have to keep the good stuff hidden."

That was true. I had a black-market shop of my own. A place I used to pour my heart and soul into. That was before my appointment at The Judas Agency. Now I seemed too busy to even keep my own place running.

"Not just the door. The supply line too."

Dan pointed over to a gadget my Agency partner, Alex, and I had set up in the corner. I had no idea how the thing worked, but it transported cases of liquid gold straight to Dan's storeroom from a warehouse I'd arranged Topside. Like I said, booze did nothing for a wayward Woebegone sentenced to an eternity in The Nine. Soda, however, that still held all its reminiscent sugary goodness ... as long as you could lay your hands on some. I, as it happened, specialized in procuring this sort of hard to find item in my off time. I kept Hula Harry's in soda, and Dan, in turn, kept the local Woebegone happy ... ish.

"Don't worry about it. Just don't get caught with that thing. If The Agency finds out I swiped one of those transporter gadgets for you, we'll both wish we were ..." I stopped short. "Well, we're already dead, but you know what I mean."

Dan nodded as he secured the secret storeroom again.

"Don't worry. They'll never find it now that you built this hidey-hole."

We strolled out of the storeroom, and a Woebegone woman walked over from a nearby table. Her eyes darted from side to side, never quite meeting anyone's gaze. A Freshborn—a Woebegone straight out of the Gnashing Fields with no recollection of who she was or how she got here. Every Woebegone cycled through the Sulphur Pools over and over each time they died in The Nine. They suffered a perceived eternity in unending pain and suffering only to be reborn right back here in The Nine, clueless and vulnerable. It made them ripe for any lowlife to pick up as something known as a Disposable—a slave to be used and reused again and again for any number of horrible atrocities.

I had a friend who had made it her mission to rescue as many of these Disposables as possible. I kept telling her she couldn't save them all, but she was stubborn.

"Dan, this is Rita. Another one of Zoe's rescues. Can you give her a job here until she gets back on her feet?"

I gestured in her direction, making her flinch, then lowered my hand in a more careful motion. "It's ok. We're here to help. We're not going to hurt you."

She still wouldn't meet my eyes. "Okay."

It was all she said before taking a step back to clasp her arms across her body in apprehension.

"Sure. No problem." He motioned for her to follow him. "Come over here, and we'll get you started."

They went behind the bar, and Dan introduced her to another woman. Another Freshborn further on her way to recovery.

A motion at the front of the bar caught my attention, and I looked up to see my partner, Alex, come through the door.

"There's a firestorm on the horizon," she announced. "If anybody wants to scurry home, you better make a run for it now. That smoke front isn't waiting for anyone."

CHAPTER TWO

Alex's announcement of an impending firestorm brought a round of cheers from the crowd of Woebegone inside the bar. Not the sort of reaction one might expect for a storm that dropped flaming brimstone and slag hot enough to melt your face off.

A firestorm was the dark side's way of keeping things fresh in The Nine. By fresh, I mean killing two thirds of the Woebegone unlucky enough to be caught out in the open without shelter.

"You wanna help me with these doors?"

I glanced over to see Dan carrying a heavy, steel beam. I shuffled forward and grabbed an end before I realized what the huge chunk of metal was for.

"Drop your end into the hooks and then help me with the other one."

We dropped the beam across the reinforced automobile doors he had fashioned into his entry, and it dawned on me that Dan was locking out any Woebegone left outside the bar.

"Hurry up." Dan struggled with a second bar, this one even

larger than the first. "As soon as those Woebegone see that firestorm, they will overrun this place like ants."

I looked around the bar as I helped him secure the last brace and then lock a shutter over the window. The place was busy but by no means full. A pang of guilt punched me in the gut. Dan had one of the few reinforced structures in The Nine. The cars stacked on top of one another formed a shelter about as bombproof as anything above ground. It had endured many firestorms, protecting those inside, unlike the ramshackle shanties that stood beyond. I had a similar luxury at my shop. It, too, was reinforced with angle iron and steel, and I, too, locked the place up tight every time a firestorm blew into town.

"What are you doing? Woebegone are going to die out there." Alex glared at the two of us standing next to the door. She wore her usual outfit. T-shirt, vest, jeans, and boots, all riddled with holes to display her ivory, tattooed skin. She had her blue hair tied into a ponytail, keeping it all out of her face and making it impossible for me to avoid her scowl.

"The second he opens that door, it would be a free for all in here," I said. "Don't forget where we are and what sort of Woebegone inhabit most of the landscape outside. This isn't Heaven, and those are not the pearly gates. Give them a reason, and there would be an all-out turf war to command ownership of this shelter."

Alex's eyes went back to the door again. She knew I was right but didn't like it any more than I did. The current patrons all mingled together to form one big group. It reminded me of the hurricane parties I had seen on the East Coast. Gatherings to witness the incoming doom, only this time, they would be the only safe ones while everyone outside died. Their cheery disposition made me want to throw them all outside too.

"Come on." Alex grabbed my arm and led me over to a couple of empty stools at the bar. "Let's grab a drink and wait this thing out. I have some news that might cheer you up."

I did my best to sit/lean on one of the stools. Dan had hand made every anti-ergonomic monstrosity himself. They were misshapen, chrome monoliths that had no business holding the human form. I had never worked out whether he was a horrible craftsman or a master at practical jokes. Maybe it was both. Either way, the stools were about the most uncomfortable things anyone could ever sit on.

"What happened in here anyway?" Alex tried to lower herself onto a stool a couple of different ways then gave up and just stood next to the bar. "Looks like a firestorm swept through before I got here."

"Bunch of college kids on a bender. You know how it is."

"A bar fight?" Alex's mouth dropped open. "And I missed it?" Alex was by far the best hand to hand fighter I had ever seen. If she had been here, I could have sat back on my anti-stool and watched the show without lifting a finger.

"Should've been here ten minutes earlier. They would have been all yours."

Alex huffed. "I'll bet you used your Knuckle Stunner."

I stammered. "There were like, twelve of them. I had to help out Dan. Look at him." I motioned toward the frail looking man at the other end of the bar. Alex quirked a half smile and crossed her arms over her chest.

"I'm sorry if we aren't all quadruple-black-belt-super-ninjas like you. Didn't you say something about news?" I turned toward the bar and sulked. Alex let me sit there a moment then let out a laugh.

"I'm sure all *twelve* of them are wishing they had picked another bar to cut up in about now." She jabbed my arm, giving me a little shove when I didn't respond.

"Are we pouting? I bet a throat punch would turn that frown upside down." She said it as if she were cooing to a baby, grinning like a mad woman as she drew her hand back and balled up a fist.

I covered my throat with both hands and pinned my chin down at the same time. "I am not pouting. And why would you even think of something like that?"

Alex giggled again. "Well, you're not pouting anymore."

I relaxed ever so slowly, keeping my eye on her hands. "Are you going to tell me your news or what?"

Alex grinned and bounced on her toes, brimming with excitement—an action so unlike her, it felt a little disturbing.

"I just came from The Agency, and it looks like we are off assignment for a while. We have no official business to attend to."

I tilted my head. "So, what does that mean? We're on vacation?"

"Better." Alex's smile grew even bigger. "We get to freelance."

I blinked. "I still don't follow."

Alex rolled her eyes. "When we have free time like this, it's a chance for us to make a real name for ourselves at The Agency."

Suddenly, I didn't like where this was going.

"So, what do you have in mind? I hope it is nothing big. I am pretty busy helping Dan around here."

Typically, a comment like that would wipe the smile right off of Alex's face, but today it didn't even make a dent. I definitely didn't like where this was going.

"We can't sit around drinking Coke all day if we want to keep our jobs. We're expected to get creative and come up with a project on our own. I did some research and found the perfect thing for us to work on. It's quick, destructive, and doesn't require a lot of manpower."

I raised an eyebrow, inviting the inevitable answer.

She grinned. "You and I are going to derail a train."

CHAPTER THREE

"Are you crazy?" My voice raised about three octaves and got loud enough to hush a few of the closer conversations. I cleared my throat and started again, trying not to shout in Alex's face.

"There is no way I'm going to go up and murder a bunch of people traveling on a train just so we can make headlines in the company newsletter." I scowled and shook my head at her. "Frankly, I can't believe you're willing to do something like that either."

Alex groaned. "Don't get your Boy Scout sash all wrinkled. I'm not talking about a passenger train. I want to hit a freight train. No one on board but an engineer and a conductor."

I narrowed my eyes. "That doesn't seem like a headline worthy event. What's the catch?"

This time Alex hesitated, looking up at the ceiling as if the answer might float down to her from the thick, metal sheeting. "You may not like that part as much. I want us to hijack a hazardous cargo train, derail it in a town, and cause some major chaos."

"What? That's no better than the passenger train."

"Sure, it is. People will have time to get out of the way—for the most part. If the railroad is on the ball, they should be able to warn the town long before it hits."

"Are you sure about that?" I said. "What if it piles up on Main Street with no one the wiser?"

Alex slapped her hand down on the counter and turned to face me. "We are expected to orchestrate our own missions at times like these. You should be happy I didn't come up with a way to wipe out a football stadium or a major city."

I stared at her in disbelief. I had worked with Alex for a while now. We had been through some crazy situations together, not all of them good, but she had never leaned the way of a typical Judas Agent. They were all about death and destruction, but Alex had a heart. At least, I thought she did. Even considering something like this made me think I may have misjudged her this whole time.

Alex looked away, and, in that moment, I knew I was right. She played the part of a hardened Judas Agent, but deep inside beat a heart bigger than anyone I had ever met. I just had to help her remember it.

"We're doing this." She straightened, stiffening her resolve before I could say anything else. "I will do all the research and legwork, but you're coming. You owe me, and now is the time to pay up."

I grumbled something unintelligible, and she snapped a backhand into my sternum, causing me to buckle over.

"I'm sorry?" She cocked her head to one side as if she were straining to hear me. "Did you say something, partner? Something like, 'Yes, of course I'll have your back the way you've had mine every time I've had some half-baked idea to run our mission into the ditch?' Is that what you were going to say?"

I groaned. Much as I wanted to support her, I wasn't just a Judas Agent. Judas Iscariot had personally recruited me into his organization to do the opposite. I was a double agent, part of his Denarii Division, which prevented the very worst catastrophes from ever happening. Alex knew nothing of this, of course. She believed I was a Boy Scout in wolf's clothing. In a way, I guess I was. The problem came with the fact that Alex kept getting sucked into my Good Samaritan activities. Not helpful for her or her career.

Alex turned her gaze back on me again. It felt like a two-hundred-pound bag of guilt dropped into my lap.

I sighed. "All right."

"All right, what?" She kept her ear cocked toward my mouth, waiting to hear the words.

"All right, I have your back on this one, just like I always do."

Her eye roll would've impressed every teenage girl within miles.

"Look, I just don't want a bunch of people getting hurt. I may have earned an eternity in Hell, but I'm not a monster."

"And I am?" Alex backed off and glanced up at me. "How about if we find an empty cargo train and then derail it way out in the middle of nowhere? We can even make sure the conductor and engineer jump off in time, so no one gets hurt."

A little bit of that guilt bubble began to dissolve at this idea.

"Yeah," I smiled and nodded. "I could be on board with something like—"

"I was kidding." Alex shook her head. "Figures you would want to do something like that. What good is a train derailment if nothing is destroyed? It would be like robbing a bank before anyone put any money in it. What's the point?"

"I still don't see why we have to do something so destructive," I grumbled. "We could spend our time doing something more constructive. Like digging around and find out what Simeon's up to. Don't you want to know why he possessed the body of an autistic genius to control a cancer curing nanotechnology? We're the bad guys, remember? He can't be looking out for the greater good. We can see what he's really up to, yank him out of Ryan's body, and stop whatever crazy plan he has for the world."

Simeon had been our last mission, or at least the disastrous results of it. He was a loose end the way Rapunzel had hair, and I couldn't let go until I caught up to his game. Alex looked like someone had hit her in the face with a wet gym sock, and her face continued to contort as the silence grew.

I couldn't take it anymore. "What?"

She took in a deep breath and gritted her teeth. "How does that stupid-ass plan fit into the mission statement of The Judas Agency? This place is called 'The Disaster Factory' for a reason." Her voice got louder as she inched closer to me. "Disaster being the key word. What you just described is called, hhhhheeeellllllppppping. We are NOT agents of the rainbow-land unicorn coalition; we are Judas Agents! Now act like one!"

I leaned back and put my hands up. "Ok, ok. You're right. I was just wondering—"

"Stop! I don't care what you are wondering. I don't care what Simeon is doing. I told you. This is a chance to make a name for ourselves, and that's exactly what we're going to do." She let out an exasperated breath while she closed her eyes.

"Okay, I get it. We have a job to do." I tried to keep the cynicism out of my voice but didn't quite succeed. Alex either didn't notice or decided to ignore it.

"The bad news is we don't have much time to do it." She winced as she sat down on the bar stool next to me. "If Sabnack sends us out on another mission, we won't be able to pull it off, and it'll be a missed opportunity."

I raised my head, seeing a glimmer of hope. If I could drag my feet and cause Alex to miss her window ...

"And don't think you are going to drag your feet and try to slow me down either." She eyed me. "I'm onto your good guy tricks. They won't work."

I tried to look abashed. "I told you I was on your side. I can't believe you think I'd—"

"Yeah, whatever. Just don't try to derail my plans."

"I see what you did there."

"I was waiting to use that one." She smirked. "Seriously, though. I need this."

I nodded, feeling that guilt bubble grow even heavier. "Don't worry. I'll help however I can."

It was a lie, of course. I had already decided if there were a way to stop her I would, but I had to figure a way to do it without jeopardizing her position at The Agency or our partnership. All in a day's work in the Denarii Division.

"What can I get you two?" Dan set two glasses down in front of us and leaned into the bar.

"How about some of the good stuff," I said.

Dan reached down and pulled out a fresh can of Dr. Pepper. About as rare as rare got in The Nine. Dan had all the booze anyone could want, but it didn't do any good. It tasted terrible and never got you drunk. Hangovers were still a thing though. I could never figure how, but drink enough hooch, and you would go straight from sober to hangover city. Hell definitely had a sick sense of humor.

Dan poured the soda. I took a long pull of the fizzy liquid.

"Thanks, Dan." Alex raised her glass to him. "The place looks great. It's really shaping up in here. Pretty soon, you'll have more business than you know what to do with."

A crash signaled the arrival of the firestorm outside. Storms always started with thick droplets of molten fire then graduated into boulder sized brimstone raining down. For those stuck out there, it would be like dodging a lava machine gun during a smelting rockslide. The lucky few inside got to listen to the carnage firsthand. No matter what kind of Woebegone were out there, I cringed every time another brimstone crashed into the building.

The patrons began to twitch as well. They had lost their boisterous laughter and seemed to wonder if Hula Harry's would stand up to the pounding from outside.

"Don't worry," Dan said. "This place has been here longer than most of you. Relax and have another drink."

The crowd of Woebegone loosened up a little at that, and Dan turned his attention to us again. "Kids don't understand how lucky they are right now."

"At least you have a safe place to hunker down," Alex said, finishing her drink. "I'm glad you were here. I can't remember the last time I was out in something like this."

Firestorms conveniently missed The Judas Agency, always skirting around the borders of the compound, so Alex had likely missed out on firestorms for quite some time.

"It's been nice while it lasted." Dan pulled out another can and filled our glasses with a second dose. "You may as well drink these up. Between you and me, in a week Hula Harry's is going out of business for good."

CHAPTER FOUR

"**W**hat do you mean shut down Hula Harry's?" I slammed my glass down a little harder than I meant to. "You can't shut down! This is the one safe-haven Scrapyard City has. Woebegone can forget they're in Hell while there here, even if it's just for a little while. That's no small thing."

Dan clamped his pipe in his teeth and then went back to drying a set of highball glasses behind the bar on the towel he always had slung over his shoulder. "It's not as if I want to close the place down." He scrubbed at a particularly stubborn spot, scrutinizing it under his squinted stare. "I don't have a choice."

"You don't have a choice?" I wanted to throw my glass across the room. "I've worked my tail off the last few weeks setting up your secret storeroom, and I stuck my neck out arranging that black-market supply line for your soda."

"I never asked you to do that for me. That was *your* choice. Don't get me wrong, I appreciate it. But..."

"But what?" I looked over for some backup from Alex who still nursed her Dr. Pepper like a high dollar scotch.

"What do you want me to do about it?" she said. "It's his place."

I pinched the bridge of my nose and did my best not to scream then looked up at Dan again. His methodical way of drying his glasses was about to drive me over the edge.

"And what about them?" I motioned to the Woebegone behind me. "You've built up quite a following over the past few weeks. What was the point of all that if you were just going to shove them out the door next week?"

Another series of booms announced a barrage of brimstone bouncing off the reinforced walls of the bar. The Woebegone I had motioned to were gathering closer and closer together, like sheep seeking safety from a wolf—carrying a flame thrower.

"It does seem a little strange," Alex said. "If you weren't ready for this, why did you work so hard to set it all up?"

Dan peered out at his frightened patrons and sighed. "I know you haven't been here long, but have you ever wondered why a place like this exists? More importantly, why it's allowed to exist?" Dan stacked his glass on a pyramid behind the bar then picked up another and started buffing it to a shine as well. "Look at us. We should be out in that storm, dying like all the other Woebegone, but here we are, sitting in a bar, drinking soda, and having a good time. Those Woebegone behind you were enjoying themselves too."

He stopped drying his glass for a moment and eyed us as if his point should be obvious.

"We're in The Nine. Having a good time is not on the menu."

I had never considered that. My shop was small, so it flew under the radar. Hula Harry's was big enough to put a Quick-E-Mart to shame. Any Hellion would be obligated to tear the place down out of sheer principal.

"So, what's your secret?" I asked. "How do you keep the place running?"

Dan's eyes went up to his other patrons to make sure no one

was listening, then he leaned into us and whispered. "I pay off a high-level demon for protection."

Alex's mouth fell open. I was less shocked. After all, I had dealt with the underbelly of The Nine for years, and that meant I had made deals with demons too. Alex had either been kicked around on the streets as a Disposable or sheltered by The Judas Agency. Below board deals with demons were not in her forte.

"How do you pay? I mean what could a demon want that ..." Alex tried to work it out in her head, but it wouldn't quite compute.

"I think what she means is, a Hellion can get pretty much anything he wants anyway. Why would one want something from you?"

I already knew the answer, at least in general terms. Dan must have a connection Topside, a way to procure items the Hellion couldn't acquire otherwise. I worked my shop the same way. Offer something shiny and afterlife could be a whole lot easier.

Dan's eyes went up to his patrons again. They still huddled in the middle of the floor even though I could hear that the firestorm was already subsiding. The wall shuddering booms had withered to stuttering bangs.

"I shouldn't say, but considering the circumstances ..."

Dan paused a moment then went on.

"My business associate has an affinity for clowns. The rarer and creepier, the better. I procure paintings for him in payment for keeping this place up and running."

"Clowns?" Alex's eyebrow shot up in disbelief. "Are you serious?"

"As a stroke patient," Dan smiled. "He even has John Wayne Gacy as his personal henchman. Keeps him dressed as Pogo the Clown."

I screwed up my face in disgust. "Gacy, the serial killer?"

Dan nodded. "The very same. Considers Gacy his most prized possession."

"Okay, that is sick on so many levels." Alex shivered.

Gacy had been convicted of several murders along with having an affinity for luring young boys into his home. He also had a side gig as Pogo the Clown, where he worked charity events and children's parties, presumably where he scouted out his next victims. He had finally been caught and put to death in the Illinois penal system. A ready-made minion for an evil clown-loving demon if I ever heard of one.

Alex took another swig of her soda. "So, what happened? Why has anything changed?"

Dan's lip curled up in an expression of anger and disgust. "This last delivery was a special request, so I had to convince my Topside contact to steal it from a private collection. Wasn't easy, but I got the job done."

I stared at the unassuming man before me and marveled at the contacts he must have to pull off such a feat. They had to rival my own black-market dealings. I wondered if he even needed my soda supply trick or if he would've found a way to get it on his own.

"I don't understand," I said. "If you got the painting, what's the problem?"

"Problem is, I don't have it anymore. Some two-bit thief carried out a smash and grab on my place and took it. If I don't produce the painting in five days, Gastrith will tear the place apart with his own hands."

"Can't you file for an extension or something? Maybe this, Gastrith, will listen to reason?"

Dan shook his head. "I think he would get as much pleasure tearing this place apart as seeing his precious painting."

"If only there were someone around who could look into the stolen painting for you." I looked up at the ceiling as if I were trying desperately to come up with an answer. "Two people who work for an agency with significant investigative power."

"No, Gabe." Alex's eyes shot from me to Dan and back again. "We can't get involved in this. We have another project to work on, remember?"

She reached for my wrist, but I managed to pull it out of her reach before she could twist it into some sort of ninja pretzel roll.

"Come on. You have to admit, it's nice to have a place to come and hang out. Plus, the locals love it, and it gives Zoe's rescues some place to work. I promise it won't take any extra time. At least no time away from your project."

That was a lie. If everything worked out the way I wanted it to, we would find the painting, save Dan's bar, and run out of time to finish Alex's train crash all in one fell swoop. I couldn't ask for anything better.

"I can't offer much." Dan hit her with the puppy dog eyes. "But as long as I'm open, you'll always have a place to hide from firestorms and bureaucracy, not to mention all the soda you can drink."

I gave Alex my best doe eyed expression as well. She caved within seconds.

"Fine. But this better not interrupt our other mission." Alex finished off her Dr. Pepper and pushed the glass toward Dan again. "Your list of IOUs is growing. Both of you."

I nodded and pushed my glass toward Dan again as well. "Guess you better tell us everything you know about Gastrith and his freak show clown collection."

CHAPTER FIVE

T he next morning, I made my way up to the cubicle sea of grey personality assassins Alex called an office area. The Judas Agency had spared no expense in laying out a labyrinth of identical cubes the color of depression and suicide. A box of crayons would run for their lives if they ever caught sight of this place.

The long trek to Alex's personal work coffin took me several minutes. Somehow, the inner space of the floor seemed to outdo the outer expanse of the building. Searching for her cubicle always took far longer than logic dictated it should. It didn't help that every wrong turn brought me back to a break-room full of Kale doughnuts. Even they were a little grey.

I was just about to give up when a shock of bright blue hair caught my attention.

"Could you put up some kind of sign or something when you know I'm coming by? Maybe a big, red arrow?" I rounded the corner to Alex's space and saw her typing away at her computer. "I know it would be against the color code around here, but it would make finding you a whole lot easier in this ocean of office prisons."

Alex spun in her chair, meeting me with a smile gleeful enough to make me fall back a step.

"Stop complaining. At least we're inside a building and not out with the creepers in Scrapyard City."

"Hey, you're talking about my home, you know. I have quite a few friends among those creepers."

Alex rolled her eyes and turned back to her computer. "Whatever. It's about time you got here. I've been doing research for our little side project all morning. I have a lot to show you."

I groaned inside, wishing she had said almost anything other than that. I never thought I would wish so hard for an assignment to come down from above. I didn't want to deal with any sort of catastrophe, but anything would be better than an idea that Alex cooked up. This train thing was all her. She owned every bit of it, and worse, she seemed to be enjoying it.

"Sit down." Alex motioned to a chair next to her desk with a nod. "Let me show you what I've got so far."

I sank into the chair and leaned into her desktop so I could see her screen. "Are you sure we should go through with this? Maybe we should take a step back and—"

"I'm sure." Alex cut me off fast enough to blunt a meat cleaver. "I've made a list of possibilities and narrowed them down to these six rail lines. They're all leaving within the next three to four days and have one load of hazardous cargo or another."

Every word that came out of her mouth turned my stomach into a pit of writhing snakes. I had spent almost every moment since the day Judas had summoned me to his office feeling guilty because I had to lie to Alex about my true position in the Denarii Division. I had jeopardized her job more than once to prevent The Agency from carrying out one atrocity or another. I regretted every lie because I believed deep down she was a good person stuck in an impossible position. Now I questioned that belief. How could she be good inside and still be willing to hurt so many innocent people?

I leaned in to examine the trains she had listed on a sheet, still finding her willingness to go through with this plan hard to believe.

"Each one of these could be derailed in locations that would do a significant amount of damage, it's just that ..."

She hesitated, and I turned my gaze from the computer screen to her eyes. They were unsure and full of doubt, but also full of determination and malice.

"It's just that what?" I prompted, hoping she had second thoughts about the whole thing.

"It's just..." She sighed. "The only places we can derail these trains are in heavily populated areas, and I know you'll throw a fit about pulling something like that off. So, it's a great, big problem, that's what."

Alex crossed her arms over her chest and stared at the screen, refusing to meet my stare. I fought to keep a smile from creeping onto my lips. I knew she had a heart in there, even if it wanted to use mine as a scapegoat.

I looked back at the screen, bypassing all the trains she had chosen, and looked for something different, something that might work for the both of us.

"There." I pointed down further on the list at a coal transport train scheduled to depart from Portland in two days. "What about that one?"

Alex snorted out a laugh. "That train transports nothing but coal from a mine in Montana to a seaport in Oregon. It wouldn't even be loaded. It'll be an empty cargo train headed back to the mine to pick up another load."

I looked at Alex and raised my eyebrows. "No hazardous cargo to cause mass casualties. I could sign on for that as long as we pull the engineer and conductor off."

"When I suggested derailing an empty train in the middle

of nowhere, I was only kidding. This is no different than dropping a bomb in the middle of a desert. If there are no people around to see it ..."

Alex paused and seemed to work something out in her head. Her sudden change of heart did not give me the warm fuzzies.

"Hold on a second." She turned to her computer, moved her hands around like she was conjuring some sort of voodoo magic spell, and brought up a map of a railroad. It ran all the way from the coast to the coal mine, passing through several smaller towns along the way ... and one larger one.

"Bozeman, Montana." Alex proclaimed and punched her finger at the screen. "There is a bend in the line right in the middle of town and a switching station a few miles ahead of it. We can catch them when they stop to switch crews, pull everyone off, and let her rip. The train will hit this curve full speed and bam, derailing catastrophe."

Alex looked over at me and threw an arm around my neck, pulling me in for a hug. "Thank you for this. It's a great idea."

I put an arm around her to sort of half hug her back while my brain franticly tried to backpedal out of the hole I had dug myself into.

"I didn't mean we should ..."

Alex sat back and turned to the screen again. "This is perfect. I really thought you were going to try and stop me. I even considered talking to Sabnack about ..."

Alex pulled up short, not finishing her sentence.

"Talk to Sabnack about what?" I asked.

"It's not important now. I was wrong. Let's just focus on this mission."

I stared at her. "You were going to ask for a new partner, weren't you?"

Alex didn't answer which was answer enough for me.

"That's great." The pang of disappointment that punched

me in the gut was hard to ignore. "You weren't even going to tell me?"

"I'm sorry. It was selfish. I got so obsessed with this whole freelancing thing, and I thought you wouldn't go along with it. Then I grew a conscience and couldn't even go through with the original plan myself. Then you come up with this."

She smiled, holding her hands out to the screen as if it were a finished masterpiece. "It's just bold enough to make a statement without creating massive destruction."

"Derailing a train in a town is pretty massive," I said.

"You know what I mean." She beamed. "Casualties will be at a minimum, and it'll still be seen as a success."

Alex threw her arms around me again, pulling me in tighter this time. I couldn't help but be distracted by her body so close to mine. I fumbled my arms around her while trying not to seem like I wanted to hug her too much, even though that's exactly what I wanted to do.

Alex straightened and smiled at me. "I'm sorry for even thinking about a new partner. It won't happen again."

I shot her a sideways smile. "You say that now ..."

Alex laughed. It was a musical sound that made me tingle all over. I decided to drop the train discussion and try something else.

"So, just how powerful is this search program of yours?"

Alex eyed me, picking up on my sudden change in subject. "This is The Judas Agency. It is the most powerful information gathering system in the world. Why do you want to know?"

I shrugged. "Could it look up a former client? Maybe the head of a cutting-edge medical company who happens to have a grudge against The Judas Agency?"

Alex shook her head. "No, we are not doing that."

"Come on. Let's see what our old friend Simeon Scott is up to nowadays."

CHAPTER SIX

"No way. What's with your obsession with that guy? Let it go." Alex pushed me away from her desk and hit something on her keyboard that made her computer screen go black. "Simeon Scott is someone else's problem now. It's bad enough the way we let that mission end. I'm not going to stick my nose into that hornets' nest to get stung again."

Alex and I were supposed to make sure a nano-tech company brought a revolutionary new medical treatment to market. That was weird enough—The Judas Agency making sure something good happened in the world. That's when Simeon Scott stepped in. He was a Judas Agent with a bad reputation. Simeon had found a way to possess the autistic genius who had developed the revolutionary advancements. That, combined with a tragic accident that killed the CEO of the company, put Simeon firmly in the driver's seat. Oh, and if that weren't enough, Simeon used to be a part of the Denarii Division. Disavowed, presumably for his betrayal. Yeah, nothing to be curious about Simeon at all.

"Come on. What can it hurt to do a little inter-web-net investigation?"

Alex snorted. "Did you just call it the inter-web-net?"

"You know what I mean."

"It's called the Internet." She grinned.

"Whatever. Don't you want to know what he is up to? Why would he resurface now, and how did he manage his possession trick? That isn't something that happens every day."

Alex stared back at me without saying a word. After a few seconds of tortured silence, I sat back in my chair. "Fine, if you won't do it for Simeon, do it for Ryan. He's a good kid, and he had his body hijacked by some power-hungry lunatic."

Ryan was the Autistic savant Simeon chose to inhabit, pushing Ryan ... Well, I wasn't sure where that put Ryan, and that was the point. Ryan was an innocent, and I didn't like the thought of his mind being held captive while Simeon used his body like a cheap suit.

"At least find out what's going on up there for Ryan's sake."

Alex's eyes softened, and her shoulders fell. "I liked Ryan too, but that doesn't give us the right to barge into their business. If Ryan's still in there, he would've surfaced by now, and I would've seen it."

Alex held her mouth open a second too long, as if she were rewinding her words in her head, then she clamped her mouth shut and looked away.

"What do you mean you would've seen it?" I leaned in close to her, trying to catch her wandering gaze. "How would you know if Ryan had surfaced or not?" I sat back and smiled. "You've been spying on him, haven't you? You've been spying on them, and you didn't tell me. Admit it."

Alex threw her head back and let out a breath. "Fine. I didn't tell you because I knew you would get all weird about it and want to do more. And clearly, I was right. Yes, I've been following Ryan ... Simeon on the Net, but nothing odd has happened. MiRACL is growing by leaps and bounds, and their nano medical technology is spreading all over the globe.

Simeon is using the company to help millions. I saw an article talking about the fact that he's given away as many treatments or more than people have paid for. He is a worldwide hero."

I shook my head. "How does any of that make sense?"

Alex shrugged. "I don't know, but it's true. Looks like Simeon is one of the good guys, even if he did inhabit an innocent to get a second chance at life."

Alex's gaze fell to the floor as she considered something. There was more to the story between her and Simeon, I just didn't know what it was. I did know that Simeon had no business existing Topside or anywhere else for that matter. When an Agent betrayed the Denarii Division by revealing its existence, their soul was forever banished to the nowhere realm of the Denarii.

Turned out nowhere wasn't all that forever after all. Point was, Simeon knew the Denarii Division's secrets, and he held that fact over our heads. He wanted to be left to his own devices, which made me want to know what he was up to even more. It couldn't be good. It was all more than my curiosity streak could handle.

"Well, I, for one, don't buy it," I said, breaking her trance. "We should go up and pay him a visit. See what's going on for ourselves."

"And that is exactly why I didn't tell you about my little spy mission. I knew you would get all crazy and want to take things to the next level. Leave it alone. Sometimes things are just what they seem to be."

"And sometimes they aren't. What's with you and this Simeon guy, anyway? How do you know him, I mean really?"

Alex kept her gaze on the ground. "I told you. I only know *of* him. Just his reputation, that's all."

"But when we saw him, he recognized you. There must be—"

Alex stood up from her chair and grabbed my hand. "Enough of this Spy vs. Spy stuff. Let's get out of here."

I stood up as well, not missing the sudden change in subject or the fact that she was holding my hand. She led me into the walkway. It felt like wading into the middle of the deep, grey sea again. "Where are we going?"

"Don't you worry about that. I have a big surprise for you. Say what you want, The Judas Agency looks out for its own, and it's about time they started looking out for you too."

CHAPTER SEVEN

"Okay, open your eyes."

Alex pulled her hands away from my face, and I looked around, not knowing precisely what I was seeing. We stood in a long hallway carpeted in a deep burgundy, and the walls were lined in a fabric of the same color. The entire space had been dampened so much that sound felt like a sin. Each wall contained a honeycomb of hexagonal windows about twice the size of a manhole cover, and I could see odd footholds jutting out between them to allow access to the windows higher up. They were stacked four-high and stretched about as far as I could see, but not one of them seemed to offer a view to the outside of the building.

"I don't get it." I ducked to peek into the closest window. "Where are we?"

The glass was tinted, preventing me from seeing what was on the other side, deepening my confusion.

Alex skirted around me and pulled on a small handle to a window located at shoulder level. As I peered inside, it reminded me of an MRI, or maybe a casket, or a mix of both. The opening sunk into the wall about seven feet and maintained its hexagonal shape. The walls were lined with more fabric, and there were small shelves located on either side. The bottom was padded with a thin mattress, and there were fresh linens and blankets folded up neat enough to be in a cruise cabin.

"Is this some sort of suspended animation torture? It looks like Dracula's hipster nightmare come true."

Alex punched me in the ribs, knocking the wind out of my cynicism. "This is a standard issue Judas Agent apartment. Yours is number 316." She gestured to the numbers stenciled above the window in looping script. "It's a safe place to sleep, read, whatever, and I stuck my neck out to make sure you got one."

I pinned my forearm to my side, trying to stabilize the pain from her jab, and looked in again. "My mistake. I must have had something in my eye. It's lovely. Thanks for thinking of me."

Alex slammed the window/door to the sleeping coffin and turned to leave. "You're impossible sometimes, you know that?"

I reached out to grab her arm. "I know. I'm sorry." She stopped pulling away and turned around to look at me. I made an over dramatic show of nursing my ribs. "You just caught me a little off guard, that's all."

She looked down at my side and poked at me with her finger. "If you want, I can make the other side match, so you don't have to walk all crooked like that."

I straightened immediately and dropped my arm. "Nope, all of a sudden, I'm feeling much better."

I shot Alex a grin, but she didn't return the sentiment. "If you don't want the apartment, tell me now. I'll turn it back in, so they can give it to someone who'll appreciate it."

I sighed. "I said I was sorry. What do you want? I'm used to staying in my shop. I know Scrapyard City isn't uptown, but at least I have a little elbow room."

"Yeah, you get to rub elbows with the nicest rapists and murders. I can see why you wouldn't want to give all that up."

I groaned. "Okay, I'll give it a shot."

"Don't do me any favors. If you want to sleep in a cesspool, that's your business. I was just trying to do something nice for my partner."

I dropped my head in utter defeat. "And I appreciate it more than I can say." I looked up at her and took her hand in mine. "Thank you very much. I really do appreciate it."

Alex softened a little and pulled her hand out of mine. "All right, now you're laying it on a little thick. Bathrooms are down the hall. You'll find a locker inside corresponding to your apartment number. You can keep your stuff in there at night."

I eyed the tiny space again, trying not to look as skeptical as I felt. "Got it. Where's your apartment?"

"It's past the locker rooms on the women's side." She pointed down the hall. "After our workout, I'll show you your office space and get you going on a computer. You'll have to learn how to work one without yelling at it."

"Be still my heart. A sleeping coffin and a place to kill my soul too. You really are good partner."

Alex drew back her fist for a low jab. "It's not too late for that matching ribcage."

I stepped back and held up my hands. "Just offering a compliment, that's all. See what I get for trying to be nice?"

Alex turned to walk away for real this time. "Just get to the gym. You didn't even try to dodge that poke to the ribs. We have a lot of work to do."

I let her get several strides away then said, "It was a lucky shot. You'd never get it in again."

Alex turned on her heels, but I was already headed off the other direction. She would just have to wait until we got to the gym. I wondered if they had body armor in the locker rooms.

CHAPTER EIGHT

When I walked into the gym, Alex was already practicing her katas on the mats at the far side of the room. She wore her usual workout clothes, tight shorts and a sports bra that exposed the many tattoos covering her supple skin and hard muscles. Watching her like this short-circuited every wire in my body, and I had to rein in the impure thoughts that inevitably surfaced.

I forced myself to look away toward the other Agents who worked out in different areas of the psychotic training layout. The Judas Agency didn't believe in weights and stair-climbers with convenient cup holders for your squeezy bottle. They took more of a survival of the fittest track on the whole fitness idea.

A large portion of the gym was dedicated to a demented sparring course full of spiked pitfalls, boiling oil, and pointy posts. I would kill myself just walking on it, much less fighting within its fatal confines. I had seen Alex go to work there once, showing off her graceful and deadly moves against an opponent. It was a sight beholden to see, and one I never wanted to experience first-hand.

There were sections dedicated to Hellion weapons training,

equally as inhospitable, where participants could unleash slightly less lethal facsimiles of the real working weapons upon one another. I watched as a new sparring match got started. There were two guys on the floor, and one of them, a twenty-something with crew cut blond hair and a sleeveless T-shirt, held my favorite weapon, a Whip Crack. It was essentially a bullwhip crossed with a chainsaw, and I had one of my very own. A black-market acquirement that had served me well over the years. It could tear pretty much anything to shreds, especially a bad guy begging for trouble.

Here in the gym, the Whip Crack didn't have its teeth, but it was still a steel sheathed bullwhip. Not exactly foam rubber nun-chucks.

Crew Cut went to work on his sparring partner, slashing his whip out in a wide arc. His partner came in low with some sort of weapon I couldn't see, but Crew Cut was too fast for him. He brought his Whip Crack around and back down, tearing into his partner's thighs with a snap. Partner went down, and Crew Cut went in for the kill. Had that been a working version of a Whip Crack, his partner would now be devoid of both his legs. As it was, Crew Cut had one more shot at him. He brought the Whip Crack back and then swept his arm forward again. His partner tried to slip out of the way, but he never stood a chance. Crew Cut's weapon reached out and slashed his back as he tried to retreat, opening up a gruesome wound.

Partner let out a shriek and collapsed to the floor. Crew Cut just coiled up his Whip Crack as if he were putting away an old extension cord, hung it on the weapons wall, and walked away.

Agency attendants appeared from somewhere and collected Partner with less sympathy than I would have thought the guy warranted and hauled him off in the other direction.

I continued across the gym to where Alex stood in the middle of her practice mat, peering off toward where the fight had been.

"Remind me never to partner up with that guy," I said, trying to break the tension now permeating the room. Pretty much everyone had stopped to watch the gruesome spectacle. There weren't many people in the gym, but half a dozen Agents were getting back to their workouts, looking higher strung than they had a few minutes ago.

"That guy walks around here with his ego in a wheelbarrow." Alex looked disgusted. "I'd like to see him challenge me to one of his little sparring matches."

"Why does anyone climb in there with him if he has a reputation as being such a douche?"

"He either suckers a new guy or pisses someone off so bad, they lose all sense and step in anyway. Truth is, he's got some talent. There aren't many Agents who could teach him a lesson, not that he would learn anything."

"Good thing I have a badass partner who can punch a hole into an engine block." I lowered my voice for effect and held up a single fist. "With her bare hand."

Alex laughed. "You may not count yourself so lucky after we're done working out."

She turned and walked to the center of the mat. I put my hand down and followed her. We faced each other, and Alex raised her hands in a fighter's stance.

"Show me what you've got."

Normally, it would be against my every instinct to hit a woman or even try to hit a woman, but Alex was different. She was a weapon in her own right. If I did manage to land a punch, it would be cause for either celebration or panic. I had yet to find out which.

I sunk into my own fighter's stance and threw out a few feeler jabs. She blocked them with ease. I feinted to the left, trying to draw her off with a fake jab, then came around with my right. Alex fell for none of it. She spun, trapping my wrist in her hands, then slammed me down to the mat like a fat sack of doughnuts.

I rolled over to peer up at her. "I thought I had you that—"

A foot crashed down next to my head then Alex drove a fist down to within a millimeter of my face.

"Your enemy is not going to laugh and exchange witty banter when he throws you to the ground. He's going to come in hard—go for the kill. Your jokes won't protect you from any of that."

Alex stood up and retracted her impending hammer blow. Even though she never made contact, I couldn't resist rubbing my nose as I got up next to her, trying to ease my bruised ego.

"You made your point," I said. "Save the *punch*-line for later."

I smiled, and for a moment, I thought Alex might add her punchline to my face after all, but she stood back instead and glared at me.

"Your cousins almost killed you a few months ago, and they weren't the only Woebegone in The Nine who know how to fight. No partner of mine is going to be a wallflower who gets his ass handed to him every time things get a little rough."

Alex took up a fighter's stance again. "You can either take this seriously and try to learn something, or I will make it necessary for you to learn out of sheer survival. Your choice."

I held my hands up in surrender and took a step back. "All right, I'm sorry. I was just trying to untangle your bunched up ..." I decided not to finish that statement. "Maybe you could show me that throwing move you hit me with."

Alex huffed and straightened. "Fine, but if you don't stop punching like a preschooler, all the throws in the world aren't going to help you."

"Ouch. I think I liked it better when you were hitting me in the face."

"We can switch back. It's way more fun for me too." Alex

tried to keep a straight face, but I saw the grin hiding beneath the surface.

"No, that's all right. Let's give your fists a break."

Alex walked me through the throw technique several times at slow speed, adjusting my feet, hips, and hands each time. After about a half an hour, I became fairly competent at it.

I tossed Alex to the mat, and she rolled to her feet for the hundredth time.

"Not bad," she surmised. "Keep practicing that footwork, and you'll be able to pull that off in your sleep."

I raised an eyebrow. "A compliment? Are you feeling okay?"

Alex backhanded me in the stomach. "I read it in a book somewhere. Compliment children and they're more successful."

I covered up my stomach and let my mouth fall open in astonishment. "You read a book?"

I dodged her next swing, grinning as wide as she was. "Not to change the subject, but what are you doing this afternoon?"

"Why, you going to take me out for a hot date?"

Something inside me pinged with panic. Alex must have seen it in my face because she laughed and shook her head. "Calm down, cowboy. I'm only kidding. What do you have in mind?"

My nerves had shifted into a spin cycle, and I had no idea why. If I were alone, I would slap myself in the face. Alex was my partner. Why was I getting so worked up?

I did my best to tamp down my nerves and flatten my voice. "I didn't want to say anything in front of Dan, but I may know a guy we can talk to about that stolen painting."

Now it was Alex who looked like she had been caught off guard. "How could you know that? I planned to do a little digging on my computer this afternoon, but I haven't had a chance."

I smirked. "No offense to your computers, but I've been

networking relationships down here for almost forty years. I've learned who to talk to and who the major players are. We just need to find them."

Alex looked me up and down as if she were sizing up a prize piece of beef. This did nothing to help my post-pubescent nerves.

"All right, Columbo." She turned around to pick up her gym bag and towel. "Let's go talk to your snitch."

CHAPTER NINE

Our first stop was my black-market shop. It had been my home for almost forty years, and while it was fairly new to Alex, she had still been here enough to think of the place as a sort of unruly relative. Rough, ugly, and occasionally host to some unpleasant characters, but loved, nonetheless.

Zoe leaned out of the front window and met us with a wave and an over-eager smile as we approached. A sure sign that she was more than happy to see us. She wanted something.

"What a nice surprise. You never stop by the shop anymore. I was beginning to wonder if you remembered how to find the place."

I cringed at the accusation. Zoe had all but taken over my black-market operation. We traded high value items for secrets. Both were priceless in The Nine. I had built the place with my own two hands. Had developed relationships with the Woebegone and Hellions who learned to trust me. It hurt that anyone, even a friend like Zoe, might be settling into my position because I couldn't be there.

"I planned on stopping by as soon as—"

Zoe cut me off. "I'm just giving you a hard time. I realize

you're busy. Besides, I like having the shop to myself. It's sort of turning into a place I can call my own. I'm thinking off adding some curtains and maybe an accent wall for color."

"Ouch." Alex shot me a wry grin. "Sounds like the homestead is getting along fine without you. You're going to have to take up knitting or do some cross stitch to stay busy if this keeps up."

I turned a narrow-eyed glare to Alex, trying to act as if her words didn't hurt. Zoe must have seen through to my frustration because she reached out and laid a hand on my arm, offering a genuine smile. "I'm kidding. Don't worry. The place will always be here for you when you're ready to come back. I'm not jumping into your shoes. Just adding another pair, that's all."

I offered her a crooked grin in return and nodded. "Thanks for taking care of the place. I'm sorry I haven't been there more often. With The Agency and helping Dan at Hula Harry's, I've been swamped."

Zoe held up a finger. "Speaking of Hula Harry's, did you get a chance to introduce my friend, Ruth?"

Her over-eager smile returned with such force it drew a laugh out of Alex standing next to me.

"She just needs a place to stay until she gets her memories back." She started before I could say anything else. "I found her outside the Skin Quarries. I couldn't leave her there. They would have locked her up with the other Disposables."

"You found her outside the Skin Quarries?" My eyebrows went up in question, and Zoe looked away.

"I may have found her just inside the warehouse ... inside a cage. But it was unlocked, so she was practically free."

The Skin Quarries were the largest dealers of Disposables in the area. They also ran a nightclub known as the Wax Worx where they used their Disposables for heinous entertainment for The Nine's elite. It was by far the worst place I had ever seen or even knew existed, a true model of Hell.

"You have to stop pulling Woebegone out of the Skin Quarries. I know you want to make a difference but ..."

"But what? Management is a joke now that your cousins are gone. I could waltz in there and free every one of them if I wanted to."

My cousins had run both the Skin Quarries and the Wax Worx up to a few months ago. At least until Alex and I had paid them a visit and aggressively reallocated their management.

"So, what if you did? Even the clowns who run it now would replace every Freshborn slave within a week. And what would you do with the ones you freed? Hundreds of Freshborn Woebegone wandering the streets of Scrapyard City? It would be a free-for-all. They would be no better off than they were in the Wax Worx."

Zoe hung her head. I waited for the usual arguments in response. She would never let it go. She had been one of them, at least until I saved her. Now she saw it as her personal mission to save every other Disposable who walked The Nine.

"You're right."

I turned to peer at her, but she did not raise her head to meet my eyes. "Come again?"

She waited a beat, then repeated herself. "I said you're right." This time she looked up to meet my surprised expression. Even Alex had her mouth halfcocked in disbelief.

"This is never going to work." Zoe's eyes were bloodshot, but the tears that threatened to fall had not touched her cheeks. "I can save one Disposable after another. I can save them all, but it won't stop. There will always be more. More Disposables, more handlers, more lowlife scum looking to use them."

I hated to see her like this, but she needed this reality check to make her realize the truth. We were in Hell. Bad things were a part of our existence. A big part. All we could do was try to make small adjustments. Help one at a time and make a Woebegone happy for a little while. We were never going to fix the system.

Two women ambled out of the hidden storage space at the back of the shop where we stockpiled our trade goods. It was also an excellent spot for eavesdropping.

Jazzy and Meg were the first Freshborns Zoe had saved, and the three of them had been inseparable ever since. Jazzy, a Latino jackhammer who could handle pretty much any situation, and Meg, a fire engine red head with attitude to match, never left Zoe's side. They came out to stand by her now. They acted casual and didn't say a word, but I knew they were ready to jump into Zoe's side of any argument.

Alex stepped forward and put a hand on her arm, softening her gaze into understanding. "Look, it might feel like you're giving up but—"

Zoe shook her head and pulled away. "I said you were right. I didn't mean I would stop fighting. I just need to think bigger."

"Wait, what?" Alex turned and raised her eyebrows at me.

"Saving one or two Woebegone will never make a difference. I need to think bigger. Hit them where it hurts." Her grin turned manic, and she hurried around to the shop door and came out to face us.

"I gotta run." She hopped up to kiss me on the cheek then pulled Alex in for a quick hug. It all happened so fast neither of us thought to stop her, and Zoe began to jog away as if she were late for an all-expense paid shopping spree.

She turned as she went, twisting to glance back at me one last time. "You really should stop by and say hello to some of the locals. They miss talking to you. I'll see you both soon."

Zoe hurried off down the street, and Jazzy and Meg wandered out the door to watch her go as well.

"Hold on. That's not what I meant." I shouted the sentiment

way too late. Zoe was not only out of earshot, she was almost out of sight.

"Well, that was some smooth talking."

Alex crossed her arms and stared at me. After a moment, Meg and Jazzy did the same.

"What did I do? I just wanted to keep her out of trouble."

"That's sort of the problem." Meg spoke up. "The more you try to big brother her, the more she tries to prove she doesn't need it. Let her go. She'll figure things out, and she has us to watch her back. Nothing's going to happen to her."

Now it was my turn to level a cynical stare in their direction. "Like the way you kept her from being held captive at the Wax Worx?"

The three of them had bitten off way more than they could chew a few months back, requiring Alex and I to come to the rescue. All five of us had come close to punching a ticket to the Gnashing Fields that day. Not one of us came out of it unscathed.

"That wasn't our fault," Jazzy said. "There was a lot more to that mess than we expected, and you know it."

She was right. My cousins for one. They had wanted revenge on me for killing them in the real world, among other things. Taking Zoe as bait had been an easy way to make sure I showed up for the party.

"I would love to stand here and debate family politics with all of you, but we did come here for a reason, right?" Alex raised her eyebrows in that way that said if I didn't pull my head out she was going to pull it out for me—in a very undignified fashion.

I nodded and let out a breath. "Great. I got so off point I forgot to ask Zoe about our contact."

Meg and Jazzy both relaxed and dropped their arms.

"What contact?" Meg asked. "We're here almost all of the time. Maybe we can help."

I glanced at Alex, and she shrugged as if to say, "It couldn't hurt."

"We're looking for a guy named Marcus. He's in and out of here every once in a while and has contacts in some of the darker merchandise channels down here. He usually wears a nice kicks and beanie."

"Yeah, I know that guy." Jazzy stepped forward and leaned up against the front of the shop. "Zoe met him the other day. Said he's hanging around the fetid district. Not a nice place."

"What place is?" Alex huffed. "Do you know if he's still there?"

"Maybe. They made a hefty deal, I know that. She took a lot of our stores and wouldn't let us go with her. It all sounded pretty under the table."

I shook my head, resisting the urge to go off on an overprotective tirade.

"Thanks. If Zoe comes back, try to keep her out of trouble, will ya?"

Meg laughed. "Sure. Bring me a set of angel wings and a halo, and I'll jump right on that."

Alex and Jazzy laughed. I tried to join in, but the sound came out more like a grumble. I couldn't help it. Zoe was like family to me, and the thought of her in trouble was never funny. I just had to hope she had enough brains to steer clear of anything that could get her hurt. If history were any indication, hope and brains wouldn't even keep her from knocking at trouble's door.

CHAPTER TEN

A lex and I strode our way through a jumble of rusty angle iron, old sheet metal, and dark windows. The alley represented everything your mother said about shortcuts and strangers, only this one was in Hell, and the strangers were more than just strange.

"You sure know how to show a girl a good time." Alex kicked a roll of mangled chicken wire out of her way. "Next time maybe we could tour some of Jack the Ripper's favorite hangouts."

"Don't worry," I said, keeping my head on a swivel. "People know me from the shop down here. No one's going to mess with us." My eyes went to every doorway and window anyway. There was little light to see inside any of the makeshift hovels, but I didn't want some Woebegone thug catching us by surprise any more than Alex did.

"Besides, you brought your death sickle thingies." I motioned to the weapons she had hidden up the loose sleeves of her long, black coat. They were a sort of dual switch bladed set of Kamas she could draw like derringers at an old west poker game. They popped into her hands faster than a spring-loaded ace, and she rendered a shave and a haircut in a way only Sweeny Todd could appreciate.

"They are Song Reapers, and if you call them death sickle thingies one more time, I will reap that smile right off your face."

I held my hands up by way of surrender. "I'm just saying you are overdressed for the occasion." I motioned to the ultra-fashionable spy duster she wore. "There's nothing to worry about down here. You can depend on me."

Alex eyed me, and my hand went into my pocket where I had stowed my Knuckle Stunner. Known or not, a little more caution couldn't hurt.

We rounded a corner and saw a group of Woebegone huddled over a greasy fire in a fifty-five-gallon drum. None of them spoke, but the misery they shared was written all over their faces. Cold in The Nine was something Alex and I didn't have to worry about anymore. As Judas Agents, that particular torture had been suppressed. Every other Woebegone in The Nine felt it though. That frigid, miserable chill that originates deep in their bones. That shivering misery was one of the greatest tortures of our forsaken afterlives. Nothing they could do would take that chill away, and nothing would stop them from trying either. I had dealt with it for four decades, so I knew all too well how they felt.

I recognized a face among the trio and raised a hand in greeting.

"Marcus, my friend. We've been looking everywhere for you. What have you been up to, buddy?"

Marcus, the Woebegone in the middle, was wrapped in an old, wool blanket and wore a dirty, red beanie and fingerless gloves. He took one glance at us and tore off at a dead sprint.

"I can depend on you, huh?" Alex shook her head and took off after him, her duster billowing behind her. I followed suit with much less flair. Marcus tripped and jumped his way through a minefield of debris littering the narrow pathway between the tall shantied structures. Everything from old bicycles to beer cans to I-beams blocked our path. The U.S. Marines Corps couldn't have set up a better obstacle course.

I leapt over what appeared like the remains of an old railroad bridge while Alex clambered around an old section of chain link fence. Marcus had obviously mapped out the most efficient way through the web work of steel because despite his gangling technique, he was pulling away. If I hadn't been up on high ground when he slipped in through a side door, he would have made a smooth escape.

Alex had sprinted ahead, so I whistled to get her attention.

"Hold on." I dropped off of a jutting steel grate that led to nowhere and landed in behind her. She eyed me with more than a little irritation until I motioned to the door Marcus had disappeared into. "He went in there."

Alex looked at the door then at me. "How bad do you want to talk to this guy?" She put a hand on the door, holding it closed. "We could walk into anything in there. He might be long gone out the back door anyway."

I smiled. "I'm sure this is some sort of misunderstanding. I've known Marcus for a long time. He probably has a good reason for running. I bet he got spooked and wanted to talk to us in private."

Alex raised an eyebrow. "Yeah, I'm sure that was it. Marcus tore down this street like a cat with its fur on fire because he wanted to chat in a more romantic location."

"I didn't say romantic." My hand went to the door handle, and Alex removed hers. "I said private. I'll bet he's right inside."

Turned out I was half right. Marcus stood on the far side of the room, but the place was anything but private. The smallish hovel seemed to be some sort of hangout. I would call it a bar except for the lack of booze—or fun.

Six patrons stood from their makeshift tables the moment

we walked into the decrepit establishment, and Marcus grinned. It was not an evil smile, but rather an expression that said you really shouldn't have followed me through that door.

"I told you so." Alex had taken up a semi-defensive stance to my left, and I could tell by her posture that she was ready to draw her Song Reapers and go to work.

"Take it easy," I whispered. "I got this."

Alex glanced up at me then straightened. "Fine. You go handle your buddies over there, and I'll wait. Show me what you've got, tiger." She crossed her arms and made a show of leaning back against the wall. Suddenly, the room seemed a lot more crowded.

I turned my attention from Alex to Marcus again.

"Hey, man, why did you take off like that? I just wanted to ask you about ..."

I took a few steps in his direction, but the wall of Woebegone closed in around me until I could no longer see Marcus.

A big guy with a scraggly beard and an arm full of tattoos poked me in the chest. "Why don't you take your girlfriend and go back to your shop?"

Tattoos poked me again and moved forward, forcing me back a step. The wall of Woebegone moved with him.

"What's with the hostility? We just want to talk to Marcus. I know him." I hopped on my toes trying to see over the barricade of grimy fat and muscle. "Tell them, Marcus. We go way back."

Tattoos poked me again, furthering his advance. "One last chance, then we're going to help you out that door in pieces."

I glanced over at Alex. She looked bored, leaning on the wall examining her nails.

"I could use a little assistance here."

Alex peered up at me then over at Tattoos and his crew. She seemed to size them up for a moment then walked toward the door. For one stomach-dropping second, I thought she might leave me alone with all this bad breath and sweat, but then she stopped and threw the bolt on the door, locking it in place. Tattoos and his crew stared at her, and frankly, so did I.

She, in turn, went back to leaning against the wall again and shot me a rueful grin.

"Like you said. You got this."

CHAPTER ELEVEN

W e all stared at Alex for a beat. They probably wondered if she was serious. I did too. It only took half a breath to realize she was not only serious, she had no intention of helping me. This would be sparring practice on steroids, and if I didn't jump first, it would be over before the fat man screamed.

I spun on my heel, whipping the Knuckle Stunner out of my pocket. In my haste, I hadn't laced my fingers into the loops. The resulting catastrophe was my only weapon flying across the room only to land at Alex's feet. She put a toe on it, holding the electrified knuckles in place as she continued to examine her nails. She made no move to return them.

Her stocking would definitely be full of coal this year.

Tattoos saw the exchange and grinned. "What's the matter, girlfriend got your toy?"

I spun and charged him without saying another word. Alex had punished me with a face to face Muay Thai headlock for weeks until I had learned it for myself. It served me well now. Tattoos weighed way more than me, but if I had his head, he would go anywhere I pointed him.

Tattoos breathed heavy into my face and tried to break my grip on his neck. I knew if he did, it would all be over. His henchmen did their best to skirt his now flailing feet to get at me, but I kept jerking Tattoos left and right, keeping his blubber between them and me, adding in a knee to Tattoos' nose whenever I got a chance. It didn't take long for Tattoos to go down, leaving me with five.

Without their fat-full leader blocking their path, all five bum-rushed me at once, making it easy to toss a chair at their feet and tangle them up. They all went down in a mess of legs and elbows, and I went in for a cheap shot on the front two. A roundhouse kick and downward fist were all it took to put them out of commission as well.

Right when I began to feel good about the lessons Alex had been giving me, one of the three stood up and held the last two back. He took on a fighting stance that said he was not a blubber-filled punching bag like his predecessors. He was short and stocky, and his open shirt revealed an ocean of ripped abs above his waistline.

Show off.

As if that weren't enough, Abs lashed out with about a thousand jabs and followed them up with a flying roundhouse kick sharp enough to slice a newspaper. If I had been anywhere near him, my torso would have been a boneless side of beef. Even Alex took the time to stand up and take notice.

I raised my fists and waited. Abs somehow managed to flex every muscle in his body Bruce Lee style, then he let out a scream and charged. I had about a blink to decide how to react. I decided cheating was my best course of action. Instead of meeting him head on, I dove low and to the side, grabbing for the chair I had used to trip him and his compatriots up earlier. Chair in hand, I rolled to my feet and broadsided his head WWE style before he recovered from his charge. It was a horribly cheap shot, but it worked. Abs stumbled then he went over like a tree in the forest, skin slapping the floor so hard he sounded like a wet towel.

The last two stooges stood back with their hands held high. I guess they figured the odds were no longer in their favor. They wanted out while they had the chance.

When I didn't charge them, they both shuffled toward the door, trying to keep an eye on me and Alex at the same time. They worked the bolt free, and as soon as they had the door open, they piled out the door like a couple of loose chickens.

The moment they were gone, my eyes went to Marcus. He now held his red beanie clutched to his chest like a teddy bear. The panic written in his wide eyes telegraphed his next move so clearly a child could see it.

Alex took her toe off my Knuckle Stunner and slid it to me on the floor before he jumped. I spun and grabbed it, bringing the weapon up under his chin as soon as he made a break for the door.

"You're just going to leave after I went to all this trouble to talk to you, Marcus? That seems kind of rude."

I shoved him back into a chair and held him at bay with the Knuckle Stunner while Alex closed and bolted the door again, effectively cutting off his only escape.

With the door shut, I stepped back and let out an exasperated sigh. "What is your deal? We've known each other for a long time. What's with the tattooed welcoming committee and mister jujitsu? I just wanted to talk to you."

Alex walked over and stood next to me, staring down at Marcus with impassive eyes.

"And thanks for all your help, by the way." I switched my gaze to Alex. "That guy could've killed me."

"But he didn't." Alex shrugged. "I would have jumped in if you were dead, I promise."

I blinked at her. She did not look back at me. For the life of me, I could not tell if she was serious or not.

I shook my head and turned my attention back to Marcus.

"So, what's the problem? Why all the fighting and theatrics?"

Marcus glanced from me to Alex and back again. He glanced toward the door, sizing up his chances, then sunk in his chair when he realized they were zero.

"I figured you heard about the deal I made with your girl, Zoe."

My nerves rose to attention at the mere mention of her name. "What did you do? If she's in some kind of trouble because of you ..."

I started to step forward, but Alex put a hand on my chest. I paused, but if Marcus didn't start talking right now, Alex would need to do a lot more than put an arm out to stop me.

He must have recognized this because he sank back in his chair and pulled his beanie back up in front of his chest again, kneading it in his fingers with panicked little motions.

"Nothing like that, man. She wanted some information, that's all."

Alex kept her arm out even though I no longer pressed to get at Marcus. "What kind of information?"

Marcus looked from her to me, hesitating for a moment. So I leaned into him again, and he cracked.

"Blueprints. She wanted plans for the Wax Worx and the Skin Quarries. She said she would pay a lot for them so I ..."

Marcus hesitated again.

"Stop screwing around, or I am going to let Gabe chat about it his way."

"Fine." Marcus screeched. My anger was more show than go now, but he didn't know that. Alex did, and she knew how to play good cop, bad cop in a way I had never seen before.

"I trumped up a bunch of plans and traded them to her for three root beers and a box of Ho Ho's."

Alex whistled. "Wow. You definitely put one over on her. That's a small fortune."

"Yeah, well, now you know why I ran. I don't even have the stuff anymore. Those guys you beat up took it all from me."

I raised an eyebrow at him.

"All right, almost all of it. I kept a couple of the Ho Ho's, but that's all I can give you."

I made a show of straightening my Knuckle Stunner on my fingers then peered down at him again.

"I have a better idea. I think you're going to earn that payment with some legitimate information."

Marcus narrowed his eyes at both of us. "Information about what? I already told you, I made those plans up. I doubt real ones even exist."

I shook my head. "I don't care about that." Although I was curious what Zoe was up to. "I want to hear about a painting."

Marcus appeared genuinely perplexed for a second, then I saw realization dawn in his eyes. "I don't know nothin' about a painting. I don't even know how to paint."

"I think you're lying, Marcus. You are about to pee in your chair you know so much. Let's hear it. What do you know? Who has it? Who stole it, and how can we get it back?"

Marcus pulled his knees up to his chest and shook his head. "I can't tell you any of that. They'll have me swimming laps in the Sulfur Pools or worse. Either way, I promise it's a lot more than you could do with that little toy of yours. You'll just have to stun me. Then what? I won't be able to talk. Then what'll you do?"

Alex took half a step back and a musical little jingle came from somewhere in her coat. Before either of us realized it, Alex held one of her Song Reapers in her hand. The handle was a supple red, topped by dual black, serrated blades that arched out like miniature sickles. The weapon looked so deadly in her hand I fought an urge to step back myself.

The musical sound came from a dainty looking chain that attached the handle to her wrist, allowing her to cartwheel the blades in any number of lethal feats. I had seen her do it once. It was a sight to inspire dread and awe. Far more than Marcus was equipped to fend off with his beanie.

Alex held the blades under Marcus's chin and forced him to lift his head to look her in the eye.

"I can promise you Gabe's Knuckle Stunner is the last thing you need to worry about if we decide to cause you pain."

Marcus looked to me as if he had mistaken Alex for the good cop, but actually I was the bad cop, and she was the homicidal maniac cop.

Marcus raised a finger in the air ever so slowly. "On second thought, I might be able to help you after all."

CHAPTER TWELVE

I rattled the door to my shop, wondering why it was closed in the middle of the day, and then fumbled for the old key I kept in my pocket. "We haven't been gone two hours. Zoe has freed half the Freshborns in the Scrapyard City. You would think she could spare one to keep the shop open while she's gone."

"You want a Freshborn who can't even remember their name in charge of your shop?" Alex laughed. "I bet she's getting some air. Who would want to be stuck in this box all day?"

I glared at her, then jiggled the lock and kicked the lower half of the door, dislodging the sticky part to shove it open. "I'll bet she's nosing around the Skin Quarries. I don't know what she meant by thinking big, but I don't like it. I want to know why she tried to bargain those blueprints from Marcus. One of these days, she's going to get in too deep, and I won't be able to pull her out."

"I don't blame you for worrying, but Zoe's a grown woman. She needs to do her own thing. It's her neck to risk. If she wants to put it on the chopping block, then that's her business."

"Until it's not. How many times have we gone in to rescue her? Then all our heads are on the block."

I walked into the small shop front and unlatched one of the heavy shutters that secured the windows, pushing it open to let in some light.

"That's our choice." Alex worked the latch for the other window and opened it as well. "She's never begged us to come help her. I knew the risk when I went, and I was willing to take it. One day, I might not be. You might not either."

The thought of leaving Zoe to rot at the Skin Quarries, or worse, the Wax Worx, was more than I wanted to consider.

"I just wish she would be more careful. I can understand taking a risk, but do it for a purpose, not rescuing Freshborns when those scumbags have an endless supply waiting for them at the Pools."

"A purpose like keeping your buddy's bar open? Now, there's a cause worth dying for."

I narrowed my eyes at her. "That's different," I snapped as I hit the latch releasing the secret door to the storage area behind the shop. It was an old school bus that had been long buried beneath mounds of steel and rubble, and the door happened to open up to the back wall.

"Really? Enlighten me."

I climbed the three tall stairs, and Alex followed me in.

"Dan didn't ask for our help, and he can't do it on his own."

"Sort of like the Disposables Zoe frees from the Skin Quarries."

I grunted, knowing I was not going to win this argument.

"You're just mad because you have a big brother complex, and you can't let it go. I get it. But you need to quit treating Zoe like a child, or you are going to lose her as a friend."

I took quick stock of the merchandise in the bus, not wanting to look up at Alex. She was right, but admitting it was not on my to-do list for the afternoon.

The seats were cracked and worn but still intact. Each one held its own little treasure. A six pack of Coke, three Dr. Peppers, half a box of Ho Ho's, and the crown jewel of them all, four pristine, in the package, Twinkie snack cakes. Not bad for a hole-in-the-wall black market shop. Inventory was down a bit, but this would buy plenty of secrets. And secrets were the commodity in which this place thrived. Woebegone brought us juicy morsels to pass on to lower level hellions, and in return, we passed the good stuff to the Woebegone. Everybody won. Especially the Woebegone.

My hand went up to a locket that hung under my shirt. An Origin Artifact of great power placed in my care. Up to a few weeks ago, I had secured it in here as well, but I had taken to keeping it close. Someplace where others couldn't lay their grubby hands on it.

"I'll try to do better. It's just hard to turn a blind eye when she falls for stunts like the one Marcus pulled on her."

Alex laughed. "You mean the blueprints? Actually, I'd say that was a pretty good scam. A lot better than that shady tip he gave us about the painting. If that's not a setup, I don't know what is."

Alex sat down and lined up the Coke cans in a neat little line along the seat.

"He has no idea who stole it or where it is, but he knew where it would be two days from now?" How many thugs do you think he'll have waiting for us if we're dumb enough to show up for that one?"

Alex laughed and finished straightening her line of cans then glanced up at me to see that I was not laughing.

"Oh, you have got to be kidding."

"Between you, me, my Whip Crack, and your Rockin' Reapers, we wouldn't even break a sweat."

"Song Reapers. And you're making me sweat right now."

Alex shook her head. "And you think Zoe makes stupid decisions."

"Come on. If we're careful, we can show up and see if it's legit. If it's not, we take off. We won't even have to fight. If the tip's good, it might be our only chance to nab the painting."

I sat down in the seat across from Alex and hit her with my doe eyes.

After a second, she groaned and stood up. "Fine, we will purposely go to the set-up designed to screw us over. Happy? At least it will give you a chance to practice the moves we've been working on at the gym."

"Maybe you could help this time instead of standing there looking at your nails?"

"I doubt it." She shrugged. "You seemed so capable the first time, I'd hate to cramp your style."

I stood up behind her and followed her out of the storeroom. "The only fighting style I know is Tae-kwon-don't-get-punched-in-the-face. Team efforts are encouraged. And thanks for checking out the lead with me. I promise you won't regret it."

"Too late." She hopped down the stairs and sauntered over to one of the open windows and leaned on the counter. "What are you going to do about the shop? Zoe's still not here to keep the place open."

Frustrated, I leaned out of the other window. "I don't know. I hate to close it up again. What if someone wants to come by?"

Ales scoffed. "What difference does it make? You spend almost all your time at The Agency, and when you're not there, you're at Hula Harry's. You're not mad because Zoe's gone. You're mad because you can't be here."

The truth of that statement stung more than a little.

"I started this place, and I don't want to see it run into the ground. Woebegone come here to feel like they can do something about the horrible situation they're in. It's a tiny slice of hope in this landfill universe. I would like to see it stay open. It's the same reason Dan's place is so important. It's all about balance, remember?"

"Yeah, I remember. Speaking of balance, I need to get back to The Agency and do some more research on our little side project. That train is not going to derail itself. All this Robin Hood Stuff is starting to make me itch."

I laughed. "Not what I meant about balance, but ..."

"Hey, balance means there is good and bad. Our paycheck says we do the bad so ..."

I sighed and pulled the brace out of the window. "Balance."

Truth was, I needed to get back to The Agency as well. It had been a while since I had reported to the big guy. A visit to Judas Iscariot was never high on my favorite list, but I had experienced first-hand what neglecting that particular responsibility could harvest. I did not want to be a guest at that fun-filled party ever again. Besides, it would give me a chance to ask him about this whole freelancing nonsense. It still seemed ridiculous to me.

Alex pulled the brace for the other window and let it slam home before engaging the bolt. "Plus, you have a great night ahead of you."

I glanced up at her, my brow furrowed.

She let me wallow in my confusion for a second then said, "Your apartment. It will be your first night staying there." Her smile was so big it looked plastic. "I know you can't wait to enjoy that perk I fought so hard for."

I pasted on a smile of my own and nodded. "Of course. That night. How could I forget?"

I ushered Alex out of the door and wondered if I could jump back into the shop and slam the door before she turned around. She must have sensed my thoughts because she turned around and jerked me out of the door by my collar.

"Don't worry. I would never let you forget something like that. Let's get going. If we hurry, maybe we can find you a set of Agency pajamas before bedtime."

CHAPTER THIRTEEN

As soon as Alex and I parted ways, I made my way up to the top floor of the tallest building in the complex. The Judas Agency's architecture was arranged into six circular buildings forming a larger outer circle. The shortest and foremost structure was six stories tall, and each building thereafter grew by six stories of black glass and intimidation, leaving a courtyard of stone and statues in the middle. In a landscape of shantied steel destruction, the complex stood as a foreboding reminder that The Judas Agency reigned over all.

Well, almost all, and that was one thing I wanted to talk to Judas about. Of course, I would have to warm my way up to a subject like The Council of Seven. When it came to dabbling in areas that were above his head, he tended to get twitchy.

The elevator doors opened, and I stepped into the grandiose waiting room of the great betrayer. It was all dark wood, leather, and horrifying sculptures of cruelty and torture. I suppose I might become accustomed to it eventually, but that day was not today. I did my best to stare at the ceiling as I passed a new piece depicting a lion and his unfortunate human-shaped lunch. Whoever made these things needed some serious therapy.

Once I was past the kitty buffet, I set my sights on the receptionist. Both her age and her origin appeared to be the mid-fifties. She had silver hair done up in a beehive and jeweled horn-rimmed glasses to complete the angry librarian look. She always refused to tell me her name, but I did know one thing. She was Judas Iscariot's personal assistant, and anyone who could do that job was tougher than Superman's chest hair.

"Good afternoon Ms. ..."

She looked over her glasses at me the way she always did and raised an eyebrow. "What can I do for you, Mr. Gantry? I have misery requests to process, and Mr. Iscariot needs his afternoon stress break."

Her eyes perked up a little at that. "Perhaps you'd like to help. I planned on sending for someone, but I'll bet he'd love to break you."

I laughed. She did not.

"How long are we going to do this? What am I supposed to call you when I come up here?"

"I would prefer you didn't call me at all."

"Come on. How about Susan or Sarah? Janet? Ruby? Barbra? Give me a hint. Is it Rumpelstiltskin?"

"Shall I let Mr. Iscariot know you are here?"

I sighed. "Yes, please. And I'll earn a name from you sooner or later, Tonya."

I raised my eyebrows looking for a reaction. But she just hit a button on her desk, and the huge doors to my left buzzed. "You want to earn my name? You can start by delousing my cat and rubbing my feet."

I turned toward the doors as she looked back down at her paperwork, but I saw her try to hide a grin. I was growing on her. We'd be passing notes in class before she knew it.

The doors into Judas's office were another artist's horror

show with depiction after depiction of different historical atrocities. I hated to even touch my knuckles to the wood for fear some of the brutality might rub off and give me gangrene of the finger.

As usual, before I could knock, the door swung open on its own.

"Mr. Gantry, come in."

I inched my way into the huge office and sneak-peeked around the corner to where I knew his desk sat. "I hope I am not interrupting anything. No baby koala torture or puppy branding?"

"Not today, but if you're volunteering ..."

"No." I held up my hands and shuffled into the room to face the man himself. Judas always dressed in black on black—silk suit and tie with matching shirt. He wore his hair long and his beard somewhat unkempt, but his eyes could stare down a granite wall reinforced with diamond rebar.

Behind him stood his two faithful ... Actually, I wasn't sure what they were. Minions, bodyguards, friends? Two demons, both frighteningly intimidating in their own right.

Procel, on his left, was an eight-foot albino with dusky wings, mottled robes, and horns that extended high above his head. His twin red eyes looked to be made of pure fire and always seemed to flicker even if there was no light in the room.

Mastema on the other hand, was a horrifying vision of beauty and death. She perched on a pedestal to Judas's right like a bird of prey—all sharp claws, leathery wings, and shapely skin. A sadomasochistic nightmare. Her blindfold always disturbed me the most. That, and her ability to track my every step as she grinned with sharpened predatory teeth. It was as if she had to dampen her bloodlust to avoid being driven to violence by the mere sight of her prey. Every time I saw her, I had an urge to freeze like a rabbit, which only perpetuated my role as her helpless quarry. Between the two of them, I would take my chances with the giant albino any day.

"I was hoping you had some time for a report and a couple of questions. I just wanted to be sure you were up to date on all my projects."

Judas sat back in his chair and eyed me across a mile of black stone he called a desk. "Sit down. Tell me about your assignment."

He gestured to my usual guest chair. A horror all its own made of human bones and some sort of leather of which I did not want to know its origin.

I sunk into the racked skeleton and folded my hands in front of me. "Actually, that was one of my questions. It seems we don't have an assignment at the moment, and we're expected to do something called 'freelancing?'"

Judas nodded as if planning a terrorist plot for extra credit was the most natural thing in the world. "Freelancing is common among our more ambitious Agents. What did you have in mind?"

I took a breath and tried to remember that The Judas Agency was a place where global tragedy was a household name, even if Judas Iscariot had hired me to stop the worst of them from happening.

"Actually, it's Alex's idea. She thought derailing a train might be a big enough event for some of the higher-ups to take notice."

Judas smiled. "I think that is an excellent plan. A derailment will be localized yet still garner a large amount of news coverage. The mortality rate on a passenger train will be high but not worldwide. The event will avert any suspicion someone might have that you're working against The Agency as well. That many fatalities will go a long way toward hiding your identity in the Denarii Division."

My jaw came unhinged, and I couldn't seem to get it back in

place. Judas noticed this and stopped talking. His eyes began to take on that *you better explain before I use you for kitty litter* look, so I forced my lips together and tried for a coherent sentence.

"Not a passenger train! Why would you think that was a good ... never mind. Alex wanted to use a hazardous materials cargo train ..."

Judas opened his mouth to speak again, but I held up a finger to forestall the horrible image he was about to paint in my mind again.

"... but we couldn't find one suitable within the timeframe."

Judas closed his mouth, looking almost disappointed.

"We decided to derail an empty coal train in the middle of a town center instead."

Judas visibly sank, and I shuddered to think of what he would come up with on Iscariot Freelance Day. I was sure it would have something to do with evil llamas and a castration clinic.

"I suppose that will suffice. Perhaps you can arrange a reason for the town center to be—"

"No. We are not hosting a down home hoedown with a surprise train crash finale. I thought you wanted me to stop bad things from happening, not create them."

Judas leveled his stare at me, and I sucked up a bit of the upholstery between my butt cheeks. "Do not forget where you work, Gabriel. This is The Judas Agency. If you have to sacrifice a few in order to ensure you are in a position to save thousands, hundreds of thousands, or millions, then sacrifice you shall. I've said it before. This job is not a pleasant one, but the call of the Denarii is an invaluable one."

I sighed. As a berating went, that was about a Ward Cleaver as it got. Judas hadn't even gotten out of his chair. Maybe he had enrolled in some sort of Hellion hot yoga to calm his nerves. Since he was in a less than murderous state, I figured this might be a good time to hit him with my other little question.

"I did have one other thing to talk to you about, if you don't mind."

Judas's eyebrow twitched the tiniest bit in response, so I went for it.

"It's about Simeon Scott."

Judas flew out of his chair and all but launched over his desk to loom over me, putting a finger in my face. So much for the yoga theory.

"Simeon Scott is under the authority of The Council of Seven. Do not attempt to or in any way investigate his business Topside or in The Nine."

Every vein, muscle, and tendon strained under his skin, making me believe he was all but ready to jump out of it and strangle me if I said one more word on the subject.

Mastema let out a little giggle, and my eyes flitted over to her leaning forward on her perch as if she were enthralled with the machine gun scene of the Godfather.

"But he's doing positive things Topside." I was never very good at responding to nonverbal cues. "It doesn't make any sense."

Judas made two fists in front of my face, tried to relax his hands, clenched them again, and ground his teeth. If he didn't strangle me soon, I was sure he would have a stroke.

Like I said, twitchy.

"The Council of Seven is above my authority. If they discover you nosing around their charge, they will want to know why. Considering Simeon's history with our organization, that could prove fatal to our cause to say the least." Judas leaned in even closer, which by now was close enough for me to feel his breath on my face. "If I learn that you are investigating Simeon Scott, I cannot overstate the extent of my disappointment. It will be severe. It will be painful. Have I made myself clear?"

I leaned back trying to put some space between me and Judas's fists and reddened face. "As Mr. Peanut's monocle."

I am assuming this was not the sincere response he wanted as he bared his teeth in a vicious growl, then he closed his eyes to calm his homicidal nerves.

My tendency to smart off whenever I was nervous and his affinity for wanting to throw me through a window every time I did made us uncomfortable bedfellows, but we were working on it.

With each breath, Judas retreated a few inches, and I regained my fatality-free zone again, at least for the time being. When he opened his eyes, I offered him a toothy smile that felt more like the fear response to a bear attack. He closed his eyes, steepled his fingers in front of his face, and had to calm his breathing again.

Like I said, we were working on it.

When he was soothed enough to control his murderous intentions, he retreated to his desktop and leaned against it, continuing to steeple his fingers for comfort.

"I understand you have earned an apartment here in the towers."

I cocked my head at the sudden change of subject, caught my brain up, then offered a slow nod, still grinning with my teeth bared and eyes wide. "Alex went to bat for me. I have a locker and everything."

Another breath and Judas almost seemed affable. "Excellent. You should plan on staying here from now on. I think you will find the accommodations comforting, if not safe, from many of the hazards you face in Scrapyard City." He said that last part like it was a piece of rotted lettuce stuck to his shoe.

"Thanks. I am planning to stay there tonight."

I got up to leave, thinking I had done enough to push my luck for one evening.

"If I need anything in the night," Judas said just before I walked out the door, "Mastema will know where to find you."

I shuddered and glanced over at the raptureish hellion huddled in the corner. Suddenly, sleeping naked on the roof of the Wax Worx felt safer than one night rolled up in a demon hot pocket waiting for a good night kiss from Mastema.

I waved and then shuffled back out the door, reminding myself to never voluntarily visit Judas's office again.

CHAPTER FOURTEEN

Heading straight to bed after a visit with Judas was like curling up with a good book at a heavy metal concert. The two things just didn't go together, especially after that last visual about Mastema tucking me in. Forehead kisses from Freddie Kruger would be more comforting.

I had a little spare time, so I decided to go back and see if Zoe was back at the shop yet. Despite what Alex had said, looking out for her felt like the only thing I could control. Between my partner derailing trains and Judas endorsing it, I wanted to do something that felt—right.

When I arrived at the shop, it didn't look like anyone had been there since Alex and I had left. My mind began to spin and thoughts of Zoe digging the dynamic trio into a world of trouble started to bubble and churn.

There were only a few places I could imagine Zoe, Meg, and Jazzy going for this long. One was Hula Harry's, but after our last chat, I doubted they were there. That left only one place. The single most dangerous place I knew and also the one place she couldn't seem to stay away from. The Wax Worx.

If they had gone over there to stir up trouble, they may have found more than the three of them could handle. I wouldn't be able to rest peacefully in my oversized Judas Agency comfort coffin if I didn't go see for myself.

I sighed and saddled up the wonder tricycle, ready to pedal my way down to the most horrific place in The Nine. My trike was not the kid's version of the three wheeled conveyance or even the kind animal trainers tortured bears with in the circus. This was an actual adult sized tricycle, complete with a tool/barbie basket slung between the back wheels. Zoe had dug it out for me when I gave up the Rusty Rocket, a Vespa that had moved like a greased oil can on fire and smoked three times as much. I gave it up to a friend in need, but it still stung at moments like this. Pedaling through The Nine was better than walking, but a sweet ride like my Vespa was all but nonexistent. At least I wasn't riding a unicycle.

Bile rose in my throat as the Wax Worx complex came into view over the rise. It didn't matter how much I knew, how many times I saw it, or how I prepared myself, seeing the place always punched me in the gut the way nothing else could. The design resembled a multi-angular circus tent built out of black and purple silk, but physics wouldn't allow for a normal tent to be this big. Large spires jutted out at random angles on top, and the multi-storied structure covered the better part of a city block. The ever-present circus-style billboard flashed and swirled the club's name, Wax Worx, in bulbs bright enough to flash burn my retinas. The only Woebegone who could miss seeing this place were blind or in space, and I bet even an astronaut caught a glimpse once in a while.

I ran my tricycle into a pile of scrap metal and covered it up so no one would take my three wheeled squeaky toy for a joy ride. It was no Maserati, but I wanted it to be there when I got out. Once the trike was stowed, I reached down to streak dirt on my face and pulled my hoodie up over my head.

My cousins didn't run the place anymore, but that didn't

mean there wasn't a Woebegone or two here who might recognize me. I had caused my fair share of trouble here. The last thing I needed was to draw attention to myself. I wanted to get in and out. Check for Zoe and her friends, and that's it. Then I would be on my way.

Something inside me wished I had strapped up my Whip Crack. I may not want trouble but that didn't mean it wouldn't find me. At least I still had my Knuckle Stunner. It would give me an edge and had the added advantage of not advertising my position with lots of body parts on the floor.

I hurried up to the door and grunted at the bouncer. He didn't seem to care who was going in or out. Definitely more lax then it used to be. Last time I had been here, it took every bit of our Judas Agency clout to get us in, and even then, we had to threaten the guy within an inch of his life. Now he just sat on a stool, half asleep, staring out at the gritty landscape. Fine by me. Easy was easy, and I never turned down a free ride.

Once inside, I realized why I never *ever* came here. The main floor was recessed into the ground, giving entrants an overall view of the place. There were a multitude of circus rings, each featuring one atrocity worse than the next. Horrors performed for the grotesque entertainment of Hellion and Woebegone spectators alike. The center ring featured three Woebegone all standing naked and entangled in endless loops of razor wire. The gleaming blades wrapped under their arms, around their necks, and tight between their legs in intimate paths of cruelty. I watched as the grates they stood on superheated, forcing them to jump and dance, digging the razors deep into their tender flesh while the bottom of their feet sizzled on the glowing metal. The crowd cheered and laughed. Some even poked at them with canes or staffs, hoping to topple them over in a whole new display of bloody horrors.

Suddenly, I wanted my Whip Crack, so I could walk down there and offer them a front row seat to a horror show none of them would forget. One in which *they* would be the headline star instead of the poor Disposables they laughed at on stage.

I shut my eyes and forced myself to look away. I had to remember the mantra I preached to Zoe. This was Hell. No matter how much I might want to, I could not save them all. I could only control the things I had the ability to change, and this place was not one of those things. I needed to find Zoe, Meg, and Jazzy, if they were here, and get out before something inside me decided this place might be something I needed to change after all.

I headed down the stairs and shoved my way through the screaming crowd, not bothering to excuse myself. No one cared. I kept my head on a swivel, searching for any sign of my friends while trying not to see what everyone else was so excited to watch.

A Wax Worx handler shoved two women in front of me. They were barely clothed in rags and tied at the wrists. The handler had a cattle prod, and I heard the snap as he forced them toward one of the far rings. My hand came out of its pocket almost out of instinct. I drove the Knuckle Stunner into the side of the handler's neck, and he dropped like liquid manure. The two women spun and looked at me, terrified and lost. No one else seemed to care.

"Untie each other and sneak out one of the side doors. Get away from this building and find a safe place to hide. Don't trust anyone but each other, understand?"

They both nodded and began working the bonds at their wrists. I kept moving. There were so many, and I wasn't there for them. I did what I could—probably too much. They had a chance, and that was all I could give them.

I continued searching the shoulder to shoulder Woebegone on the entertainment floor for any sign of Zoe or the girls. It didn't take long to realize I might never see them. There had to be hundreds of Woebegone all packed in like cattle. I could walk within a few feet of them and never know the difference. The more I thought about it, I doubted they were here at all. My imagination had likely run away with itself and had brought me along for the ride. They were probably safe in their bedrolls, and here I was, wading through the sewage of The Wax Worx for nothing.

I skirted my way to the outside of the floor, ready to give up for the evening and head back to the shop, when a door opened almost knocking me off my feet.

"Watch it." A pair of handlers, both of them NFL huge and carrying a load of attitude in each ham sized fist, poured through the door.

I ducked my head and waved in apology. "Sorry about that. Won't happen again."

I caught the door and held it for them as they washed into the crowd, parting the Woebegone like whitecaps on the sea. I almost let the door close, but caught it just before it did, suddenly realizing what was inside.

In a normal club, the door might lead to a storeroom or even a kitchen, but this one was different. It led to a supply of an appalling sort. The Skin Quarry warehouse. The place where all the Disposables were held captive before they were sold or used in the Wax Worx shows.

In the past, they had been in two separate places, but my cousins had taken over the industry and consolidated. They must have moved everything to one location. I saw the old warehouse. It was a travesty even here in The Nine, stacked with row after row of human cages, full of filth and lost souls. This however was different. This was so much worse.

It still contained rows of Woebegone trapped in cages barely fit for animals, but this new place was bigger—much bigger. I couldn't see where it ended, and the cages were stacked on multiple levels rather than one. The smell of feces and fear alone made me want to retch. These Woebegone were trapped and sold, having no idea where they were or what was happening. They were helpless and had no hope for escape, and I could not help them.

Zoe understood this in a way I never could. She had been a captive in one of these cages. Knew first-hand what it was like to be a Disposable. She wanted to free them all. So did I, but it just wasn't possible. Tears rolled down my face as I let the door close before me, helpless to stop the atrocities that only seemed to grow in this hell I called home.

CHAPTER FIFTEEN

"First night in the apartments?" A fellow Agent standing next to me at the communal sinks grinned in the mirror. "I can always tell."

I stood up a little straighter and looked myself over. "What gave me away? The company sweats with the folded crease, or my face that hasn't seen a real razor in forty years?"

The stranger chuckled. "Neither. It's that look in your eyes. Everybody has it. That expectation that everything is about to be pulled out from underneath you. I had it too. Trust me. You get to keep this one."

He turned and offered his hand. "I'm Barry. Folks around here call me 'Bear.'"

He was aptly named. Taller than me and twice as wide. No refrigerator would stand in his way, and it seemed a razor was no friend of his either. His dark skin was covered with enough body hair to insulate against an arctic winter. It was no wonder he waited to put his shirt on till the last minute. He was probably hot even with the bone chilling curse of The Nine.

"Good to meet you. I'm Gabe." I shook his hand in return.

"No cool nickname though. I make it a rule to only collect the stupid ones."

"I have a few of those myself." He let out a deep baritone laugh. "Sometimes they're harder to live down than the good ones."

"Amen to that."

"I saw you with your partner earlier." Bear nodded in the direction of the apartments. "We're neighbors. I'm in the pod just below you. If you need anything, let me know."

I gathered my things off the sink, turned to pile it all into the small locker behind me, and then slammed the door.

"I will, thanks."

I waved at him on the way out, taken aback by the normalcy of the encounter. Less than an hour ago, I had waded neck deep in the worst atrocities The Nine had to offer, and now I was chatting it up in a locker room with a guy named Bear. If my afterlife could get any weirder, I didn't know how.

I headed into the long, vast hall of the apartment area. The sound dampening effect gave me that head drenched in cotton feeling, and it made me want to tip toe rather than walk to my pod.

When I got there, I had to admit, Bear was right. Part of me kept waiting for Mastema to show up or some jack-in-the box demon to pop out and say, "Just kidding," then throw me back out into the cold of The Nine.

My apartment was no suite at the Brown Palace, but compared to roughing it outside, it looked like a little slice of paradise. Very little—tiny in fact.

I managed to open the door to my pod, turn on the light, and climb up, but getting in felt like trying to slide myself into a second story sausage casing with mittens on. I wriggled and writhed, finally inching my way into the tube using the small handles provided on the outside wall. At one point, I almost fell out, evoking images of a worm monster spitting me out onto the floor because I didn't taste good. After that, I couldn't shake the feeling of being eaten. I just couldn't win.

I did my best to push the oral fixations out of my mind and tried to think of something else. Zoe came to mind. I had stopped by the shop on my way back to The Agency, and sure enough, she, Meg, and Jazzy were all sound asleep inside. I didn't bother to wake them. It wasn't their fault that my imagination had kicked off into overprotective overdrive. They had probably been running around town, turning up new clients or helping one of Zoe's Freshborns find a job. Anything but slumming it at the Wax Worx.

Still, why did she want to run down blueprints of the place? Could she be working out a whole underground railroad thing? Was she getting herself in even deeper than she was now? After seeing the Wax Worx again in all its horrific glory, anything that had to do with that cesspool seemed over her head. It was over any one person's head.

I sighed. Maybe Alex was right. I needed to stop worrying about her so much. Zoe could make her own decisions. Take her own risks. It was not my afterlife to live. At least she tried to save people rather than kill them like Alex and her plan to derail the coal train. Hundreds of people might be killed if they didn't get out of the way in time. Maybe more. I understood wanting to keep a stable position in The Agency, but this went too far. Alex and Judas could both go to ... didn't matter. I would stop that train from derailing in that town whatever I had to do.

I tossed and turned in my pod, trying to find a comfortable position. The door hung just out of reach, so I stretched out and pulled it closed before wriggling myself back into the mouth of the covers and mattress, trying not to imagine a worm gullet.

The apartment was comfortable, no doubt about it. The air smelled fresh and cool, the mattress felt soft, and the covers were warm and inviting. I felt safe and somehow exposed at the same time because I was in a place with so many other Woebegone. Either way, I suspected this would be the best night sleep I'd had in years—providing Judas didn't make good on his promise to send Mastema on a late-night visit. No one wanted that kind of teddy bear.

I turned out the light, pulled the covers up to my neck, and closed my eyes. Three seconds later, my bladder yelled at me, ensuring I would get to enjoy the whole worm eating ritual all over again before I finally settled in a second time and got to sleep.

CHAPTER SIXTEEN

Alex met me at the elevators the next morning. I stepped off into the cubicle grey wilderness and marveled once again at the contrast of her hair and tattoos to the rest of the office area surroundings. She stuck out up here like a unicorn in a New York City sewer. Somehow the two just didn't jive.

"So how was your first night in the apartment?" She crossed her arms, barring me from going any further until I gave her an answer. The smug look of satisfaction on her face told me she already knew what I would say.

I sighed. "It was awesome."

She raised an eyebrow as if to say that better not be all.

"And you were right." I groaned. "It was safe and comfortable, and I didn't have to worry about Charlie Manson sneaking in to paint the walls with my innards."

Alex smiled. "Actually, Mr. Manson works for The Judas Agency, so he has full access to the apartment areas, but try not to think about that."

I blinked.

Alex laughed. "Relax. No one messes with each other in the living quarters. It's a sort of hallowed ground. It's also a means for immediate dismissal, or at the very least, a loss of all Judas Agency privileges, and who would want that?"

"Nobody, but don't you ever worry about—" I cut myself short, cursing my tongue for running away before my brain had a chance to review the tapes.

"Worry about what?" Alex leveled an eye at me, and I knew it was too late to turn around now.

"Worry about going soft?" I almost flinched despite myself, thinking she would respond via a nonverbal communique instead. When she didn't, I went on. "I mean a guy could get used to those cushy mattresses and comfy covers. Don't you worry about losing your edge, you know, out there?" I motioned toward the untamed wilds of The Nine.

To my surprise, Alex nodded in agreement. "Why do you think I work out so hard? I keep my fighting skills sharp and make it a point to spend my fair share of time out in the waste. Staying connected keeps me from getting soft and reminds me why I do what I have to in order to stay employed here. Having a little comfort doesn't make you soft, that only happens when you can't survive without it."

I nodded. "Fair enough. I guess we'll have to keep up those sparing lessons then."

Alex huffed and headed off down one of the endless aisles of drab, grey cubicles. "After the way you handled yourself with those thugs, we definitely need to keep up the sparring lessons."

I followed her and let out a gasp. "What do you mean? I took on six guys by myself."

"Four. Two of them ran like half-starved chickens."

"Because they were terrified."

Alex laughed. "Of what? Your chair fighting techniques? I still think they were all drunk."

I glared back at her. "Not possible down here, and you know

it. If booze worked, everyone would be hammered. You just can't admit that I did a good job."

Alex shrugged and rounded a corner. "You did all right. You want to impress me, make the karate master want to beat the two starving chickens out the door."

"I guess you'll just have to be a better teacher."

That one drew an evil grin. "You remember you said that next time we're on the sparing mat."

I regretted it already.

We walked the length of what felt like several aircraft carriers before Alex stopped and presented me with a whole grey cube of my own. I wandered in and took stock of the accoutrements. A grey framed computer screen, some sort of darker grey interface hardware, a light grey desktop, medium grey walls and cabinets. The Agency had gone all in with the ultra-depression color scheme.

I sat down in the off-grey chair facing the desk and leaned back. The recline feature almost dumped me out onto the floor, but I threw my arms and legs out like a frightened cat and managed to save myself the embarrassment.

"A ninja in the making." Alex pulled up the guest chair and shoved mine upright so hard I almost kissed the computer screen.

"Pay attention. If you're going to work here, you need to be able to access the Judas Agency systems and do your own research."

Alex shoved my face toward the monitor, and I began to wonder if this would be an urban sparing session in the middle of our work area.

"I'm not blind." I tried to pull away from her, but she had a pit-bull grip on the back of my neck. "You don't have to paste my eyeballs to the screen."

"Stay still. It should be coded to your retina pattern."

"Coded to my retina what?"

Before I could finish, a bright light flashed in my eye, and the screen came to life. Alex released her cervical crippler, and I sat back to see a fresh line of text on the screen that read *Welcome, Agent Gantry. What can I help you with today?*

"Whoa, that's pretty fancy." Alex let go of my head, and I reached up to touch the screen. My finger landed on the word "today," and a hailstorm of pages popped up, giving me information on everything from today's weather, the current stock market, to the most up-to-date news.

Alex slapped my hand down like a toddler reaching for a light socket and grabbed my wrist, forcing me to hold my right hand in the air instead.

"Don't touch the screen unless you want the computer to react to whatever it is you touch. The processors will try to intuit what you want based on your past actions and habits, but until it can begin to map those out, the system will be a little erratic. For now, you can control the information content, called windows, with hand gestures, like this."

Alex balled my hand up, leaving only two fingers out and swiped them left and right. Pictures and articles on the screen began to move and respond to my movements.

"If you want something to go away, pinch it." She demonstrated with my hand and one of the pages ... windows ... disappeared.

"If you want it bigger, do this." She splayed my fingers out, and the foremost window enlarged.

"This is amazing." I turned and realized her face was inches away from mine. I became overly aware of the way her hand felt on my skin. She continued to stare at the screen, but all I could think about was the closeness of her body, her hazel eyes, and her subtle lavender scent. She tried to show me another gesture, but something went wrong. She let go of my hand, and the severed connection was enough to make me look at the screen again.

"No, not like that."

Windows began to open like the finale fireworks on the fourth of July.

"Oops." I leaned back and let Alex regain control of the runaway information while I did my best to get control of my libido. Alex was trying to teach me how to use a computer. I needed to pull it together. Handholding was a turn-on in elementary school. Calm down and be professional.

My eyes went up to Alex, bent over and sprawled out across me to access the screen in front of her. Definitely not helpful. My mind went to places that didn't involve any kind of computers ... or clothing.

I spun my chair to the side and counted wall fibers while Alex regained control of the information systems.

"All right. Why don't we start over?" Alex backed up, and the screen had changed to black again, displaying the welcome text once again.

She went to reach for my hand, but I shrugged her off. "Maybe you could just show me what to do with your hand, and I will imitate what you do."

That drew an odd look for a second, but she settled into her chair and complied. "First, what is something or someone we can search? And don't say 'Simeon.'"

She took the words out of my mouth. Fair enough. There would be plenty of time for me to do my own searching once I got the hang of this thing. "How about Zoe? We could do a background search on her. That should be innocent enough."

Alex nodded. "Okay. Hold your fingers like this." She showed me a hand gesture that looked something like hooking the air with my index finger. When I copied the gesture, a text box appeared.

"The Judas Agency servers pull from a lot more than Wikipedia and Google. We have access to everything from phone records to web histories to traffic cams. We can back-trace someone's movements through almost any point in time. Our servers save and catalog every bit of information collected from every source on the planet. The concept is almost inconceivable, yet we have been doing it for as long as man has put chisel to stone."

Alex looked at me, and I stared back at her, my hand still in the air, finger still hooked, and a blank look in my eyes.

"You have no idea what I'm talking about, do you?"

"You lost me at Waikiki."

She rolled her eyes and reached out to turn my head toward the screen. "Never mind. Just say Zoe's full name. It helps to keep a picture of her in your mind too. The system can intuit your intent through your thoughts to some extent as well. It helps to narrow the search."

I turned and looked at Alex again, hand still in the air. "You mean this thing can read my mind?" I whispered, as if that would keep it from hearing me.

"Not exactly," she said. "I'm not even sure how that part works. All I know is you enter a hard search term, like a name, and then concentrate on who it is you are looking for, and the system narrows your search into usable information rather than giving you every Zoe Grenon ever born in the history of man."

"Wow." I turned back to the screen again, over-annunciated Zoe's full name loud enough to frighten the wallpaper, then did my best to concentrate on her—definitely not on Alex—and my thoughts from a few moments earlier.

Alex snorted out a laugh. "I just told you the computer can read your mind, but somehow, you still think it's deaf."

We both leaned into the screen with anticipation. When the first article popped up, Alex squelched her giggles, and we sat there speechless.

Zoe Grenon, Indicted on Multiple Counts of Domestic Terrorism and Murder.

CHAPTER SEVENTEEN

A lex and I stared at the screen for several seconds in disbelief. I think I read the headline half a dozen times, changing the inflection on each word as if somehow that would alter the meaning. It didn't. Zoe, our Zoe, was a cold-blooded murderer.

"Hold on," Alex said, breaking the silence. "Were you thinking of her when you started the search?"

She was obviously trying to find ways to discount the impossible headline as well. My eyes went to the mug shot about halfway down on the screen where Zoe held a board with her name printed out in removable plastic letters. I pointed to it, removing any thought that this article had been written about some *other* domestic terrorist named Zoe Grenon. It was definitely about our friend.

Without saying another word, both our eyes went to the text on the screen, highlighting the story below.

Authorities today arrested a primary suspect in the Central Heights Apartment bombing. Current reports have the death toll at over two hundred. No survivors of the incident have been found. Zoe Grenon was arrested on multiple counts of premeditated murder and domestic terrorism. She is not expected to be released on bond. A connection between Zoe Grenon's family and potential gang violence may have attributed to the bombing.

The article went on to describe how an apartment building had been leveled to the ground using a series of home-made explosives. It took weeks for the authorities to sift through the rubble and find everyone. A horrific crime. Unforgivable and unwarranted.

"Trade me places for a minute." Alex stood up, no longer willing to watch this catastrophe unfold from the passenger's chair. "School's out for now. Let me show you what this thing can do."

I got up, and she sat down in my seat while I sank back into the one she had occupied a moment earlier. Her hand hung in the air and began an acrobatic routine of subtle gestures. Pictures and videos started to appear on the screen. News feeds, magazine and newspaper articles. They painted a picture of Zoe's sister, a social worker dedicated to helping underprivileged kids. She had crossed paths with a gang member and wound up tangled in violence. She lost her life trying to help him, spurring Zoe to take revenge on a massive scale. She had destroyed an apartment building to wipe out the local gang. Families died in the process ... innocent mothers, fathers, children. A few gang members hadn't been home that night. They survived. They took revenge on Zoe by murdering her family, then they had gotten to her in prison as well.

Tears welled into my eyes, blurring the words on the screen. Zoe had gone through so much. How could she have done such a thing? I always assumed her time as a Disposable had soured her spirit, but it had happened much earlier. No one could survive an ordeal like that unscarred. So much anger. So much unwarranted death and retribution. I didn't even know what to say.

Alex pulled up a series of video feeds. They weren't something any news channel could access. These were all at odd angles and often filmed with shaky hands. I recognized many of them as security camera feeds; although, I wasn't sure where the other angles had come from.

As if in answer, Alex began to explain. "These are a series of pirated videos—security cameras, cell phones, traffic cams—all following Zoe the night she allegedly destroyed the building."

I couldn't help but notice her use of the word "allegedly," proving she had as much trouble believing this as I did.

"Here she is, walking up the street."

The camera angles became fast and erratic. Some were clear, others were far off and grainy, but there was no doubt every one depicted Zoe walking up the sidewalk on a rainy night. She wore jeans and a red plaid shirt. She was soaked to the bone and kept her hands shoved into her pockets as she went. After a few minutes, she found an overhang and paused. I thought maybe she was waiting for the rain to let up, but the more I looked, the more I realized she was watching something. She stared off into the darkness, her every muscle growing tense.

"What is she—"

There was no sound attached to the video, but we didn't need it. She pulled out her cell phone, and her thumb sailed over the screen, entering a number. We could see in her face the moment the blast occurred. First, she jumped. Then a smile crept onto her lips. Then as the building fell into a pile of dusty blood and rubble, her face changed. First to horror, then sadness, then shame. She stood there watching the whole thing. She never left until the first wave of flashing lights arrived. When they did, she put her head down and headed off, disappearing into the darkness.

Alex let the image hang on the screen for a moment then pinched her fingers and closed it out. We sat there in silence. Then I sat back in my chair, running my hands over my head in shock.

"What are we supposed to do with that?"

Alex spun her chair around to face me, shaking her head. "Not one thing. We never saw it."

"What do you mean we never saw it? You don't un-see something like that."

Alex sat forward in her chair, folded her hands, and regarded me with soft eyes. "We dove into her past without asking. This is obviously something she's not ready to talk about, at least not to us. Until she is, you and I need to respect that."

I scowled and rubbed my palms into my eyes. "I just don't think I can ever look at her the same way."

"Me either. So what? Zoe's our friend. If you want to keep it that way, don't mention this mess to her. Not ever."

I groaned. "Fine."

We both sat there in silence for several minutes staring at the grey ... well, everything, then Alex stood up and smacked me on the shoulder.

"Come on. I have just the thing to get your mind off this mess."

I looked up at her and raised an eyebrow.

"Get up. We're going Topside. I want to take a look at the site where the train is going to go off the tracks."

Alex headed off without waiting for me to follow. I rested my face in my hands. How had this happened? A week ago, I would have said Zoe and Alex were two of the most kind-hearted people I knew. Rough around the edges, but they would stand in front of a bus before they let it run down a wayward kitten. Today, Zoe turns out to be a mass murdering terrorist, and my partner wants to one up her by derailing a train into a city. At this rate, I'd be bosom buddies with Hitler by dinner. I needed to figure out how to turn things around or find a way to make some new friends.

CHAPTER EIGHTEEN

"Are you trying to get worse at this?" Alex's muffled voice came through the wall as she pounded on the outside of an empty hopper car. It was the kind used to haul coal, rock, or any number of other inert commodities, and right now, the car contained me.

I tilted my head up to the sky and shouted. "It's not like I'm doing this on purpose." The echo of my voice rang inside the black walled coal car, making me sound like a whiny, prepubescent robot.

"Are you sure? Because it sort of looks like you are."

I surveyed my situation then backed up to get a run at the slanted ends of the enclosure. Two things became immediately apparent. Coal dust on metal worked something like Crisco on ice, and the slanted side of a hopper car bore a remarkable resemblance to my nightmarish childhood memories of a sun searing slide in the middle of summer playground. The second my feet hit the sloping metal, they shot out from under me, pancaking my body onto the filthy, scalding steel like a hot Gabe omelet. I half slid, half flailed my way back down, trying not to fry any more of my skin than I had to. No, it was not a major wound. And yes, it would heal, but it still hurt.

When the echoed remains of my escape attempt subsided, Alex tapped on the side of the car again.

"You doing okay in there? Sounds like you're wrestling a kangaroo ... and losing. Stop flopping around and get out here before someone sees me."

I rolled my eyes. "I'm sorry this is so inconvenient for you."

I backed up again, adjusting my acceleration and leap calculations to account for the Teflon coated man fryer and tried again. This time, I was more careful in my footing and made it three steps before my traction gave out and landed me face first onto the steel.

Fortunately, it was just far enough for me to grab onto the top edge of the rail car. I pulled as hard as I could, and a few awkward slip-steps later, I was off the hot metal and over the side, climbing down the exterior ladder mounted on the car. When I turned to face Alex, she took two steps back and burst out laughing.

"What did you do? Roll around in the coal dust before you came out?" She snorted. "You would have been better off climbing out the exhaust of a diesel truck."

I held up my hands and saw that they were jet black, along with my sleeves, chest, and pants. Even my shoes were covered in the inky dust from inside the car. "This is great. Now what am I supposed to do?"

We stood in a train yard full of cars and rows of parallel tracks. The only items we had to work with were the gravel under our feet and the open air.

Alex shook her head as she surveyed the damage. "I even showed you where to land. All you had to do was concentrate on the ground."

"Until an open rail car presented itself as a target," I shouted. "How do you ignore something like that?"

"You just have to notice it, then let it fall away. You can't let everything you see dictate where you're going to wind up in a Splice landing. Sooner or later, there will be a pool of rainwater rather than a rail car or a pile of manure. Hit that and you're toast."

Rainwater acted like a Niner's kryptonite. Something about the way we're made up or the way The Nine was put together. If we got caught in the rain or touched rainwater, it was Dorothy and the Wicked Witch of the West all over again. It only happened with the stuff straight from the sky though. Any other form of the wet stuff was fine. I tried to reason out the logic part of that whole thing, but it just made my head hurt. Instead, I made a note to remember. Rainwater bad. And don't forget it.

"Well, I can't wander around town looking like this," I said. "What are we going to do?"

Alex thought for a minute, then smiled. "Come on, I have an idea."

CHAPTER NINETEEN

Whenever Alex said she had a good idea, it usually meant the idea was good for her, not me.

"Hold your arms out wide," she shouted over the roar of spraying water, and I shut my eyes and waited for the blast.

The car wash wand she held in her hand hammered me with what felt like a thousand gallons a minute. I had to brace a foot to keep from falling flat on my back. The fabric on my coat rippled and whipped in defiance as she blasted away the coal dust. I stood in a pool of black ink as it ran down my legs and onto the concrete floor.

Alex let off the trigger and hit me in the face with a less pressurized blast of frigid water. I guess I should be grateful for small favors. I withstood the onslaught of water as long as I could, then when it began to feel more like a waterboarding than a washing, I pulled my arms in and held my hands in front of my face.

"All right, that's enough!"

Alex laughed. "Aww, come on. I haven't had this much fun since we landed in that haunted house together." She withdrew the spray from my face, aimed it at my crotch, and pulled the trigger again, blasting me again and making me jump.

"Ha, ha. You are hilarious."

Alex burst out laughing and then made a twirly motion with her fingers. "Turn around, so I can get your back."

I complied, and Alex finished my torture wash, then hung the wand back in its rack.

"Next time you have a good idea, remind me to run the other way."

Alex scoffed. "I think that was pure genius. I'll bet you're barely even damp under all that Gore-Tex."

She was right. Thanks to our unhealthy allergy to rainwater, we both had a waterproof adaptation to a Topside safari outfit. Alex wore long boots and a waterproof coat that reached almost all the way to the ground. It hung open most of the time, revealing her t-shirt and jeans, torn in just the right places to display all her tattoos.

I, on the other hand, wore a lightweight coat and pants made out of Gore-Tex. Alex had spotted the outfit in an outdoor sports store during one of our first trips Topside together. It was a patchwork of brown and orange in ways that made the manufacturer seem colorblind. All in all, I had gotten used to the odd ensemble. I thought of it as my Superman suit without the S ... or the package enhancing tights.

I unzipped my jacket to reveal the nearly dry t-shirt underneath.

"See," she said. "Now can we go check out the town?"

With all the excitement of my Chinese water torture, I had almost forgotten why we had come here in the first place. Bozeman, Montana. It was the scene of Alex's future train derailment.

She had described the place as a tiny, little, out of the way town. I would describe it as a minor city full of people, restaurants, cars, and ... more people.

As we walked along, I gawked at the size of the place. How could Alex consider this a small town? I glanced over at her. She all but skipped down the street she seemed so pleased. Then it hit me. I had no idea where she was from. If she had grown up in New York City or Downtown LA then of course this would seem like a tiny town to her. To me, a guy who grew up in the suburbs of Colorado, Bozeman looked like a virtual metropolis.

"There it is." Alex pointed across the street, and I followed her gaze to the railroad tracks several yards away. "That's the bend. The curve is even steeper than I thought it would be. Excellent." She smiled.

I looked around at all the commerce, restaurants, and roads that fronted the tracks. There was a bike path and Riverwalk that mirrored the train route and to our left, the entrance to the Gallatin County fairgrounds.

Alex took off at a slow jog toward the tracks, but a man caught my eye just outside the fairground entrance. He stood on the top rung of a ladder hanging a colorful banner. I had noticed similar signs around town but hadn't taken the time to read them. This one I couldn't miss. The huge block letters read *Fourteenth Annual Testicle Festival.*

I raised an eyebrow and couldn't resist. I walked over and peered up, trying not to distract him to the point where he fell and broke his neck.

"Hello." I raised a hand and waved.

He looked down and smiled. "You're a little early for the festivities."

I glanced toward the fairgrounds. "I guess I am. I was just passing through and saw your banners. Is this festival a pretty big deal or what?"

The man beamed with hometown pride. "People come in from all over the country. We're expecting just over six thousand this year."

My jaw fell open. "To do what?"

The man lost a little of his smile and pointed at the sign. "It's the Testy Fest. Music, beer, and good old Rocky Mountain Oysters, of course."

I made a face. "You eat them?"

"Sure do." The man laughed. "By the time the festival comes to a close, upwards of around seventy-thousand of them."

I blinked. "Seventy-thousand bull testicles?"

"We have turkey testicles too." He said it as if the statement were a normal fact, like cows have milk or chickens have wings.

"Turkey testicles?" I choked back the horror of that particular image and asked the question I feared I already knew the answer to.

"So, when is this Testy Fest? I'm in town for a few days, maybe I could stop by."

The man smiled. "That'd be great. It all kicks off the day after tomorrow. Come on by and check it out."

I nodded and started to walk away then turned back.

"This might be a weird question, but I'm sort of a train buff. I like to check out railroad bridges and snap a few pictures wherever I go. I don't suppose you have anything like that around here?"

The man's hometown pride beamed again. "Head a few miles west of town and you'll run into Strough's Bridge over Trestle Creek. It's a doozy. If you're into bridges, that one will give you plenty to look at."

I raised a hand to wave again. "Thanks, and good luck with your festival."

The man waved and went back to work on his banner. I headed toward Alex in the train yard, but my eyes remained planted to the West. If I wanted to stop this wreck from happening, I would have to find a way to get back here alone and see about that bridge.

CHAPTER TWENTY

We finished our railroad recon topside and returned to The Agency via the vomit extractor. I wondered if I would ever get used to traveling through the Envisage Splice or if I just had to live with the brain shaker aftermath. Either way, the trip back did not improve my mood. Alex remained all but giddy about destroying that happy, little town. I wasn't even sure I knew her anymore.

"Who put a hornet in your jockstrap?"

I turned to see Alex staring at me as we walked the wide hall of black marble leading away from the Envisage elevators. Unlike the rest of The Agency, this place was almost always empty. We hardly ever ran into anyone in here, making it feel like a dark, echoed mausoleum.

My face had twisted into a scowl that felt as if it might become permanent. Alex raised an eyebrow, waiting for an answer.

"You're going to paint that town in a masterpiece of suffering and destruction, and you're nothing but happy about it. I'm sorry if that doesn't sit well with me."

Alex rolled her eyes and looked away from me. "Spare me

the theatrics. We're doing this your way, remember? Small town? Empty train? Limited casualties?"

I threw my arms out to the sides. "A small town brags about the one stoplight they have on Main Street. Bozeman is a *small city*. There's a college, restaurants, apartment buildings. I bet there are thousands of people within fifty yards of that track."

Alex scoffed. "There's plenty of space between the buildings and the tracks."

I stopped and pulled her around to face me, my voice echoing off the walls as I raised my voice. "Do you have any idea how much ground a speeding locomotive covers before it stops? I talked to a guy up there who said they're having a festival that day at the fairgrounds. The fairgrounds are right next to the tracks. They're expecting six thousand people! Add that to the thousands who already live there, and this is no small-town train wreck with limited casualties."

Her expression went hazy, and for the barest of moments, I saw doubt cloud her eyes, then it disappeared again.

"This thing is going to make plenty of noise. I'm sure they'll get out of the way."

"Six-thousand people, plus everyone in the buildings, and on the street? Do you picture this locomotive crashing in slow motion?"

Alex fixed her eyes on me and poked a finger into my chest, all semblance of her smile gone.

"Look, I've tried to make this as Gabe friendly as I can. Bottom line is flower petals and free lemonade don't fit the definition of a disaster. Keeping our jobs at The Judas Agency depends on us performing this sort of event, whether it be on our own or under orders. Can't you see that I'm doing this for both of us? I'm doing my best to make sure we stay employed and out of the literal gutter."

I expected her face to be contorted in anger, but instead I saw desperation. Her pleading eyes wanted me to understand.

Begged me to agree with her. I could not. In a twisted way, Alex believed destroying that town was the right thing to do, but that didn't make it better. It didn't even make it acceptable. At least I took solace in the knowledge that I would do everything in my power to prevent the catastrophe from happening.

When I didn't say anything, Alex grabbed my arm and pulled me forward again.

"Come on. I want to show you something. I'll probably regret it, but anything is better than watching you pout like this."

I followed along, fighting an urge to glare at her every step of the way. I was *not* pouting. I felt angry, disappointed, even hurt—but pouting? That was like saying the Japanese had a hissy fit over the A-bomb. Some reactions were justified, and this was one of those times. I was about to open my mouth and say as much when Alex pulled me up short.

We stood in a narrow hallway just outside an unassuming door. Considering every other entrance in the building seemed dauntingly oversized or adorned with some sort of horrific carving, this one was a nice change of pace.

"You can never repeat what you are about to see in here. I don't know who owns this place, or even why it's here, but if anyone else finds out about it ..." Alex shook her head as if she didn't dare finish the sentence.

I held up my right hand and peered at the innocuous looking door.

"I swear, but your hiding place isn't all that hidden. I mean, it's just a door in a hallway. It looks pretty plain an all, but ..."

Alex rolled her eyes, grasped the doorknob in one hand and my wrist in the other, then yanked the door open to step inside the room.

The door slammed behind me, and it took a moment for the lights to come on. When they did, the irritating hum of fluorescent tubes filled my ears, their depressing grey/blue light flooded the room.

"A file room?" I couldn't keep the sarcasm from dripping out of my voice. "Your big secret is a room full of shelves and filing cabinets? I can see why you swore me to secrecy. You wouldn't want anyone to find out about this place."

The room stretched an impressive distance, maybe half the length of a football field, every inch occupied by grey metal drawers and manila file folders.

"Shut up and come on."

Alex ignored my growing grin and pulled me along the aisles until we got to a bank of tall filing cabinets in the back of the room.

"No offense, but I pictured something a little more snappy. Maybe a broom closet or a moldy room full of old books."

"This room contains archived records of cold case missions that were never completed for one reason or another. Missions that predate the computer, obviously. I had to look up ..." She paused. "Never mind, it's not important. But while I was in here, I found this."

She pulled a key out of her pocket and unlocked the cabinet in front of us. The lock popped out, and she gave the center handle a hard pull. Rather than a single drawer sliding out, the whole cabinet swung away, revealing a hidden doorway in the wall behind it.

My mouth fell open.

"Someone left the key in this cabinet that day, and when I pulled on the handle ..." She motioned to the open door.

When I didn't move, she waved her hands again. "I brought you all the way down here, and now you're just going to stand there like an idiot with your mouth hanging open?"

"Oh, right." I had been so stunned by the unveiling, I had forgotten to check out the prize. The doorway was small—tiny, in fact. I had to duck my head and turn sideways to get through, but once I did, the room on the other side was nothing short of astonishing.

Alex's hidden door was obviously a secret entrance to a warehouse of antiquities that would never have fit through that tiny door. Somewhere there had to be a dump-truck sized entry. Otherwise, whoever had brought all this stuff in here did it in pieces the size of a lunchbox.

"What is this place?" I whispered, not wanting to disrupt the stillness that filled the space. Dim lighting added a sovereign mood to the room, and the musty odor spoke to the age of its contents.

Alex guided me out of the way as she squeezed in behind me. "To be honest," she whispered back, "I have no idea."

She walked over to the nearest shelf and pulled down a small vase, revealing the tag tied to its base. The handwritten script read, "Joan of Arc." It took me a moment to realize Alex was not holding a vase, but rather an urn. An urn containing the ashes of Joan of Arc.

"Are you kidding me?" My eyes shot up to meet Alex's. "Didn't I read somewhere that her ashes were never found or something like that?"

"The story's a little more gruesome, considering she was burned at the stake and all, but, yes ... and there's more."

Alex replaced the urn and walked a few more paces. She passed ancient looking scrolls, small statues, an ominous looking hourglass filled with black sand. She stopped at a worn, wooden chalice covered in dust. Next to it sat an ancient looking knife.

"The cup and knife used at the last supper."

I skipped back a few steps. "Whose last supper? Those can't be the ..."

Alex nodded. "Yes. They can, and they are."

I covered my mouth with my hand and tried to comprehend what I was seeing.

"This place is filled with unbelievable artifacts thought lost in the real world," she said. "The ring of St. Edward, remnants of the cross, documents that prove fabled events in history. It's all here. All in this room."

Alex grinned and eyed the shelves with an expression of star struck wonder.

I looked around myself, unable to believe the sheer magnitude of power this room held. If even one of these items got out ...

"I don't know how this is a good thing." I moved closer to her. "The Judas Agency is holding all this stuff for ransom. They're keeping all of these artifacts from reaching the real world where they can ..."

"Can what? Prove The Big Guy's existence? Maybe, but you are looking at this all wrong. If they wanted to keep this out of the hands of the living, all they'd have to do is build a beach party bonfire. Someone has saved this stuff ... is saving it. Keeping it from harm right in the very place that would seek to destroy it the most."

My brows furrowed with confusion as I tried to work out her reasoning.

"Don't you see? The Agency ... or at least part of it, isn't all bad. Someone has the capability of recognizing the good. Saving these artifacts from what I can only imagine would be immediate destruction. I don't know who made this place, but it's a testament to anyone who tries to do the right thing."

I met her eyes and realized what she was trying to tell me. She saw this place as a testament to me. I stared at her in wonder.

"You never stop surprising me, you know that?" I reached out and squeezed her hand. "Thank you."

She shrugged, and I recognized a hint of a smile. She turned and stood next to me as we took a minute to admire the incredible artifacts around us.

"Don't forget." She nudged me with her arm. "No one can know about this place. I've never told another soul about it."

I nodded. "You have my word. I'll never tell anyone. Besides, who would believe me? The Judas Agency is storing the Holy Grail behind a bunch of dusty, old filing cabinets? They would have me committed."

Alex laughed.

We squeezed back out through the tiny door, the horrible lights of the file room singeing my eyes, then Alex put everything back the way it was.

"Hey, since we're doing a little show and tell, what do you say we take a little side trip?"

Alex looked up at me, narrowing her eyes.

"Side trip to where?"

"I haven't checked in on Dan's soda supplier since setting up that whole magic delivery thing. I'd like to drop by and make sure no one's standing there with a camera filming the disappearing cola cases."

She gave me a suspicious look. "Where's this supplier? What city?"

"Um... Denver," I mumbled.

"Denver?" She crossed her arms and narrowed her eyes into tiny, suspicious slits.

"Yeah, so?" I shrugged.

"Nice try. You just want to get close to Simeon, so you can check in on him."

"Are they both in the same town?" I tapped my chin with my finger and looked up at the sky. "Since you mentioned it, I guess we could drop in and say hello."

"No, we cannot." Alex poked me in the chest. "It's bad enough you won't back me on this train project. I don't need you actively trying to destroy our careers by sticking your nose into his business which, need I remind you, is none of *our* business."

"But what about—"

"No buts!" She reached up and squeezed my ear lobe and twisted it. "If you even think about getting near Simeon, so help me, I will cut off your ears, one-by-one."

"Wow. That was more stabby than usual." I groaned. "Fine, no surprise visits to our mysterious pal."

I eyed her as we made our way out of the file room.

"What?"

"You really didn't know Simeon? Why do I get the feeling you aren't telling me the whole truth about that guy?"

"We haven't even left, and you're already starting in on the stupid."

I shrugged and raised my hands in question. "I'm just saying it feels like you may be hiding something. You can tell me if you want to. I won't judge. If it's judge-worthy, I mean. I wouldn't do it. The judging thing, I mean."

"If I wanted you to know, I would have told you."

I brightened at her admission. "So, there *is* something. Was he your high school crush? A long-time nemesis? You can tell me."

Alex put a hand up in front of my face. "If you want to go on your little side trip, I suggest you stop asking me stupid questions."

I sighed. "I guess we can put a pin in it for later."

"If you don't shut up, I'm going to pin your lips to your—"

"Whoa, let's stop talking about pins. From now on, we use scotch tape." I waved away the visual Alex was about to paint in my mind. "No more pins and no ear-ectomys. I like my dead body just the way it is."

"We'll see." She grinned. "Speaking of secrets," Alex looked over at me and narrowed her eyes. "I've been wondering about something."

I cringed inwardly, going through a whole menagerie of potential questions.

"What's that?" I said, unable to think of a way to avoid the inevitable.

"How did you find someone to feed sodas into the transporter without giving away what it is? Didn't they get suspicious as soon as the stock disappeared into thin air?"

I laughed as we walked out of the file room and shut the door.

"That's what I want to show you. You are going to love what I came up with to solve that little problem."

CHAPTER TWENTY-ONE

"I did it!" I exclaimed to no one in particular. I examined my surroundings. My feet were not drenched in manure; I was not inside some foul dumpster. I had finally stuck an Envisage Splice landing. I had about a tenth of a second to process this victory before a jogger blindsided me like a runaway linebacker, knocking me off my feet.

We went down in a spinning heap, holding our heads where our skulls had impacted like a couple of under-ripe pumpkins. Alex appeared from the far side of a concrete rail and took in the spectacle.

"Sir, are you all right?" Alex passed me by without so much as a glance and did her best to help the other man to his feet. He wore a power jogging suit, black and grey with red pin stripes, and had a headband to match. His shoes looked like they had come fresh out of the box, and some sort of white plastic seemed to drip out of his ears like weird, white earrings.

The jogger staggered to his feet and eyed his surroundings, trying to figure out what happened. "Where did that guy come from? I didn't even see him standing there before I ..." He made a slapping motion with his hands.

I managed to find my feet as well, without any help from Alex. "Sorry about that. I was bird watching off the trail there, and I guess I wasn't paying attention. Those yellow-headed warblers will get ya every time. You know what I'm saying, right?"

Alex and the jogger both blinked at me, then Alex turned her attention back to the jogger. "My brother's a little slow. I take him out for walks, but sometimes he gets away from me. We all love him, though. He's family, after all. I'm awfully sorry."

Alex offered the jogger a sympathetic smile, then she pointed him down the path and gave him a little shove. "I don't want to keep you. Have a nice afternoon."

She waved as the jogger shudder-stepped into an awkward run again. He waved back, adjusted his drippy earrings, and loped away, power jogging suit and all.

We watched him go for a few seconds, then Alex hurried over to me in a rush. "What is wrong with you? We were supposed to land under the bridge, not on it."

She pointed to where she had emerged from around a concrete rail moments earlier. I looked over and understanding dawned on my addled brain.

"I wondered why we were landing out in the open like this." I motioned to the jogging path as though it were just then apparent that any number of people could have seen me appear out of thin air. "Seemed a little irresponsible on your part, if I'm being honest."

Alex jabbed me in the arm. "It wouldn't have been irresponsible if you had landed where I told you. No one looks under a bridge."

"Apparently, you have never seen a movie featuring a homeless person ... or a real homeless person."

Alex groaned.

"I'm sorry," I said. "I'll try to do better, I promise."

"One of these days, you are going to get hit by a car, or worse, a train." She smirked.

"You are very funny today."

"I know." Her smile widened. "So where are we going?"

I looked around, trying to gain my bearings, and saw that our landing point had put us less than two blocks from our destination. "We don't have to walk very far. My supplier is right around the corner from Simeon's building."

Alex opened her mouth in that way that said she was about to shout something hurtful, but I held up a hand to stop her.

"No visits. Just giving you a frame of reference, that's all."

I pointed to the sign on the building next to us.

Alex read it, snapped her mouth shut, opened it again, and it stayed that way as she stared back at me again.

"You can say it. I'm a genius."

Alex glanced back at the sign and read aloud, "Denver School for the Blind? Are you kidding me?"

"Where else could I find a place where no one would see the sodas disappearing? Come on. The receiving area's around back."

I hurried around the building before Alex could ask any other questions, making my way to a small receiving dock area. A thin man with dark skin and thinning whips of grey on his head moved boxes with a dolly, stacking school supplies into neat sections. His clothes looked a little too big for him, and he wore thick tinted glasses even though he was inside the dimly lit building. He always had one gloved hand out in front of him and took steps a little shorter than seemed natural, but he never wavered or hesitated in his movements.

"Hey, Ernie." I called out his name loud and clear long before we got to the dock, letting him know we were coming. He turned in our direction but didn't quite face us and offered a wave.

"That you, Gabe?"

Alex eyed me in question for a second before she came to the logical answer on her own.

Ernie held out a hand, a little too early, but I hurried forward and took it, shaking his hand in greeting.

"This is my friend, Alex."

He let go and reached out to shake her hand as well. "Sorry about the mess. I've been redecorating around here but haven't gotten the place looking the way I like it quite yet."

I laughed, and Alex let out an uncomfortable chuckle.

"I'm sorry. Just trying to lighten the moment. I like to make jokes to keep people from freaking out." He leaned toward Alex and pointed toward his eyes, "You know because I'm ... old."

This time, Alex laughed in spite of herself.

"So, what can I do for you? Or did you come by to show off your pretty friend? She's way out of your league. I'm blind, and I can still tell you that."

This time I was the one feeling uncomfortable.

"Gee, thanks, Ernie. And after I set you up with all that free soda."

"Hey, I just call 'em like I see 'em."

Alex snorted out another laugh. "You need to take this act on the road."

Ernie smiled. "Naw. I like it here. No one here to bother me, and the view is amazing." He motioned to a cinderblock wall.

I shook my head and laughed again. "All right. Stop trying to impress the girl. I just stopped by to see how things were going with the shipments."

Ernie smiled. "Everything is going great. Your guy comes by once a week. I always set aside the cases you asked for. Put them in the locker over there like you asked me to." I walked outside to the dock and opened the doors to a heavy, metal locker sitting near the building. It was big enough to hold several cases of soda. Alex walked in behind me and spotted the transporter in the bottom. She didn't say anything, but she shook her head in understanding.

"I still don't understand why your friend insists on all the cloak and dagger stuff, but he comes and empties out the locker sometime when nobody's here. I still haven't seen the guy."

"The jokes never stop rolling with you," I said, clapping him on the shoulder.

"A smile is all I ask in return."

"I'm sure you get plenty of them," Alex said.

"Let me know if you run into any trouble or need more soda. I'll make sure they keep you stocked up."

I nodded toward the door, and Alex headed in that direction.

"I will, and thanks again. Stop by anytime. It's always nice to see a friendly face."

I chuckled again as he waved goodbye and went out the door.

"What a nice guy." Alex grinned. "Although, I am not sure how I feel about you exploiting his disability to supply Dan's bar."

I did my best to look aghast. "I am not exploiting anyone. He sets aside part of a delivery, and in return, his school gets a sizable donation of sodas. Pretty much all they can drink."

"And how did you manage to arrange that? Last time I checked, The Judas Agency wasn't handing out expense accounts. How do you pay for all of this?"

I shrugged. "Turns out the regional distribution manager had a side thing going with a woman his wife doesn't know about. His old business partner is a fellow resident in The Nine. I paid him two Twinkies for some sensitive information, and next thing you know, The Denver School for the Blind has all the soda they can drink."

Alex shook her head. "Blackmail for good not evil."

"I guess that depends on your point of view."

"Looks pretty Robbin Hood to me."

We were headed up the block to the Splice point on the bridge again when someone bumped into me on the street. I turned to excuse myself and realized Alex had stopped. Her hand was inside her coat, ready to draw her gun. My head snapped to the guy who had now turned to look at us. When I saw his face, I all but fell over. It was Jake Trento, a rogue Judas Agent who had crossed our path in a bad way during my first mission with Alex. Now he faced us down out of nowhere with the living everywhere on the street.

CHAPTER TWENTY-TWO

A lex and I had foiled a plan to spread a virus across the planet that would have pretty much ended all life as we knew it. A plan Jake had been assigned to carry out by The Judas Agency. We had discredited Jake, killed his partner, and gotten away with the whole thing in the process. Jake hadn't been seen since.

Alex went for her gun, then must have realized it would do her no good. Topside injuries didn't matter much to a Niner. We healed instantly unless the wound was inflicted by one of our manifested powers—that, or a shower from above. I didn't have a rainwater grenade, so it was down to my fists and Alex's fire power. Not much compared to Jake's ability to control insects. He could call down a maelstrom of stinging, biting—or just downright creepy—soldiers in a matter of seconds.

Jake eyed the two of us, looking from one to the other and back again. He raised his hands to the sky, and I braced for a tidal wave of spider wielding hornets. Alex started to lunge, but Jake straightened and took a step back at the last minute.

"Hold on." He put his arms back down to his sides and

snorted out a laugh. "I'm just kidding around guys. Jeez, learn to take a joke."

Alex glanced over at me, looking as unsure as I was about how to react. When Jake came in for a hug, I thought Alex might lay him out anyway.

"Come on, relax. We're on the same team, remember?"

"Not really," I said. "I remember you being on team Murder the World."

Jake clapped me on the back, ignoring my statement and took us in. "You two look great. What are you guys doing here? You up top for a mission?"

Confused, I scrutinized him, still trying to get a handle on the new and improved Jake Trento. "No offense, but the last time we saw each other, the three of us weren't all that, you know ... chummy."

"Don't worry about all of that." Jake waved off our stormy past with his hand. "I'm a new man. I don't even think about all that Judas Agency nonsense anymore."

I peered at him closer. He still wore his old camouflage fatigues and hat, but he had straightened the flag on his shoulder. His hair wasn't short, but it had definitely seen a barber. And that wasn't all. Something else seemed off. He wore bandages. One peeked out from under his hat and another on his ear ... The more I looked, the more I saw gauze wrapping, tape, and band aids pasted all over his body. His hands were wrapped in several places with athletic tape, and despite the warm day, he wore his sleeves down to cover his arms, making me wonder what else was all bound up like Christmas packaging.

Alex took a step forward surveying Jake for herself. "You've been missing since ..."

"Yeah, that whole Olympics mess. I'm over it though."

She eyed the bandages and wrappings, then her eyes went wide, and she stepped back.

"You weren't missing. You never went back."

Jake smiled and pressed a finger to his nose. I swore the skin moved a little more than it should, but Jake didn't seem to notice.

"I've been living it up here in the real world." He glanced at a bar sign in the window next to us. "Let me buy you both a drink, and I'll tell you all about it."

He walked between the two of us and jerked the door open before we could refuse. I looked at Alex. "I don't know about you, but I am dying to hear this story."

"We're already dead." Alex shrugged. "Might as well hear what he has to say."

I opened the door and held it for her as she walked inside. Jake had found us a table and lined up three shots of a fiery, brown liquid as he sat down.

He raised up a glass as we took our seats next to him, and the three of us cheered and shot back the drink. Bourbon ... with emphasis on the burn. I marveled at the flavor and wondered if it would regain its medicinal qualities now that we were Topside.

As if reading my mind Jake said, "Just so you know, this stuff has all the octane it should, so be careful. Too much of the happy juice will leave you a bit legless, if you know that I mean."

Jake leaned to the side and waved to the bartender in direct contradiction to his warning. "Three more, if you please."

The bartender nodded and began working on three more bourbon bombs.

"Staying up here is the best decision I have ever made. I smoke, drink, eat, have sex, anything I want. It's all like it should be."

The bartender brought our drinks and swooped up the empties. We were pretty much his only customers, so he seemed happy to have something to do. Jake held up his glass and grinned. "To old friends, both alive and dead." Then he shot back the second bourbon like it was honeyed milk.

"Take it easy there," I said. "We're not running a race."

"Says you." Alex protested then looked back at Jake. "I don't mean to be indelicate, but, look at yourself. You're falling apart. You know ..." She lowered her voice to a harsh whisper. "Woebegone can't just stay up here. Things start ... happening."

Jake slammed his hand down on the table, and I noticed something bounce on the wood. At first, I thought he lost a coin —a nickel or maybe a wayward potato chip—but then I saw that it was something else. A thumbnail. Not just part of one. The whole thing hopping around in the middle of our table like some kind of Mexican jumping bean.

I turned my head and fought to keep myself from retching while Jake scooped it off the table and put the wayward nail into his pocket. "Sorry about that. I'll superglue it back on later."

"Superglue?" My voice shrieked the word out a little too loud. I calmed myself then continued. "How many things have you glued back on?"

Jake laughed. "A few fingernails, my earlobe. If I'm being honest that whole sex thing was a lie. I had to—"

"I don't want to know." I held up both of my hands, cutting him off before he could offer any more details.

"Don't you see?" Jake leaned in as if he had learned the secret to the fountain of youth. "None of this matters. I have a second chance to live, and I'm not going to waste it."

"Yes, but all of this is ..." Alex motioned to the ruined state of his body. "Well, it's permanent. When you die up here, and you will, you'll go back to The Nine and be reborn in the Gnashing Fields ... except all of this sticks with you for eternity. And it will only get worse. You will rot away bit by bit until there is nothing left but an excruciating monster. Don't do this to yourself."

I threw back my second shot, grateful to process this reality with a little fermented assistance.

Jake held up a finger and smiled. "I may have a solution to that little problem too. If it works, I could reverse all this damage or at least stop it from getting any worse. Any chance is better than no chance at all."

Alex downed her shot and stared at him. "You had your chance. We all did, and now we work with what we've got. Don't do this to yourself anymore."

Jake got up and winked at us both. "Don't worry. I'll be fine. In the meantime, you two take care. It was great seeing you again."

Jake headed for the door and just before he got there he turned around. "Oh, one last thing. I didn't pay for those drinks. Make sure you tip your bartender on your way out."

Jake cackled and scrambled away. I turned my head, not wanting to see if he left any body parts hanging on the handle on his way out.

CHAPTER TWENTY-THREE

Alex and I stumbled out of the bar an hour and several shots later. After Jake had left us hanging with the tab, we had to get creative. We had no cash, and the First Bank of Lucifer wasn't into free credit. The bar didn't have many patrons, but as it turned out, one was enough. Alex befriended a guy sitting alone at one of the side tables. He wanted someone interesting to hang out and drink with, and we were glad to oblige.

We fascinated him with stories of the afterlife, and he kept buying shots to make our stories all the more palatable to his unwitting ear. All said, The Nine's new Scared Straight program seemed to be a resounding success, at least until he slept it all off in the morning.

"Hold up." Alex plopped onto a sidewalk bench and put her hand up. "Hang on, I need to sit down for a sec. My head is a little..." She moved her finger in a circle. "Um... a little...spinny." She laughed.

I stood and watched her, unsure how to deal with drunk Alex. The drinks had hit me too, giving me a nice buzz, but they clearly had gotten to her more.

She patted the bench. "Come. Sit."

I did as she asked.

"Isn't this nice? The fresh air. The blue sky." She let out a breath.

We sat in silence for a few minutes enjoying the moment.

"Do you... I mean, *did* you have any smothers or sisters?" She snorted. "Brothers and ... smisters." She bumped my shoulder with hers. "You know what I mean."

I laughed. "Yeah, and yes, I have... had, a younger sister. She died when we were kids."

Alex turned toward me and pressed her lips together in sympathetic frown. "I'm sorry. I didn't know that."

"It's okay."

Alex looked away again and sighed. "I'll bet you miss her."

"I do."

"I miss my brother too." She leaned her head on my shoulder and sighed again. "I hate being dead."

I tensed at the initial contact, but my chemical inhibition made me relax again, and I just went with it.

"Have I ever told you what a great partner you are?" she asked.

"No ... never." I chuckled. "In fact, it's usually quite the opposite."

"Well, you are." She patted my leg and then left her hand on my thigh. "We should come Topside more often."

"And risk losing body parts permanently? No, thanks." Although, I could get used to her being this close to me without the face punching or ninja headlocks.

She sat up and looked at me, and I could not help but notice she kept her hand on my leg. "Did you keep waiting for Jake's nose to fall off?" She snorted. "I thought it might end up in his drink!" She burst out laughing.

I couldn't help but laugh too. Then I took her hand and stood. "Let's walk this off before we head back." I pulled her up and slipped an arm around her waist ... just for support. "Something tells me showing up to The Judas Agency like this would not be a good idea."

Alex let out a breath. "Party pooper."

We stumbled along the sidewalk laughing about Jake and the various ways he might find to reattach his appendages. A well-dressed couple passed us offering a wide berth. They probably found our staple comments uncivilized.

We turned down another quiet street and saw a familiar face exit the building ahead of us. Alex stopped and shot me a glare; an expression I would have thought impossible considering how giggly she had been. "Did you plan this?"

"No, I swear I had no idea we'd run into him." I held my hands up. "I didn't even realize where we were. Let's turn around and go the other way."

I meant it. The last thing I wanted to do was elicit a confrontation with an inebriated Alex on my arm.

Simeon Scott, or rather Simeon wearing Ryan's body, strode out of MiRACL headquarters accompanied by a thin, unassuming man I did not recognize. Simeon, of course, looked like Ryan—a Japanese American with large, round glasses and a wispy beard. Unlike our previous meetings with the true and autistic version of Ryan, Simeon carried his body in an upright, confident position. Not at all like the slumped, frightened boy he had been before.

"Hey, you," Alex shouted. "Mr. Soul-Jacking Bastard. Hold up a minute. We want to talk to you."

So much for diplomacy.

Simeon and his associate stopped to look at us.

Alex began to lurch forward, but I held her back, keeping her from launching straight at him. Since when was I the sensible one in these unsanctioned altercations?

"What did you do with Ryan?" Alex did a passible job of not slurring her words, but they still smeared together a little bit.

"Where is he now? Where did you put him? Is he in a teeny, little bottle somewhere?"

Alex made a squishing motion with her fingers and closed one eye.

Oh brother. Alex and liquor did not mix.

I did my best to pull her back and take control of the conversation. Simeon, however seemed more than a little amused.

"Alex ... and Gabe, isn't it? Looks like you two enjoyed a day on the town." He looked at me. "Good for you. Judas Agents aren't allowed enough time for R&R as far as I am concerned."

I made a concerted effort to stiffen my spine, refusing to sway no matter how much the street moved under my feet. "What about Alex's question? What happened to Ryan? He was a good kid. He doesn't deserve to be held hostage by a grease-ball like you."

Simeon crossed his hands over his heart and looked hurt. "There's no need to get personal. Ryan is right in here." He lifted a finger and tapped the side of his head. "Safe and sound."

He paused for a second as if considering his words. "That may be a bit of an overstatement. He is a quivering mass of jelly, and I could stomp him out like a bowl of grapes. But he's still in here, nonetheless."

I wanted to reach out and strangle Simeon to death, but all that would do is kill Ryan and send Simeon back to The Nine. I did not like the prospect of either.

"I suppose I have a soft spot for saving wayward souls," Simeon continued. "That's a subject you're familiar with, isn't it, Gabe? Sacrificing self for others. Saving the many at the cost of the few?"

"Don't you even talk about the—"

Simeon leapt forward and clamped his hand over my mouth, trapping my head between his hands.

"As much as I would enjoy watching you debase yourself, it would be less than satisfying to watch you do it just because you're drunk."

He looked me in the eye, and as soon as he was sure I would not say anything stupid, he removed his hand, allowing me to breathe again.

"There. Now isn't that better?"

I seethed at his condescending tone, but he was right. I had almost blown my Denarii Division secret. And for what, to hurl a few words at him? The coin would have struck me down before I uttered a single, slurred syllable.

I looked over at Alex to see that she stared daggers into Simeon's eyes as well.

"My peach. It's so good to see you. Can't we move past all this hostility and go back to the way things used to be?" He held out a hand. "Why don't you and—"

That was as far as he got before Alex pounced. She was on him like a starving monkey on a banana ... or at least she would have been.

Before she got there, the world seemed to crack, and everything vibrated into agonizing, searing sound. It wasn't just noise. It felt like a physical presence, as if someone had fractured the fabric of reality, and now it shrieked in pain. Everything blurred and hummed at an excruciating rate, forcing me to my knees as I pressed my hands to the side of my skull.

"I don't believe we've been properly introduced." The voice sliced in over the din of shrieking sound and visual pain like a hammer tearing its way in through wet cardboard. "My name is Robert Beelz. Mr. Scott is my associate and under my protection."

All at once, I realized who the unassuming man had to be. The man walking out of the building with Simeon. He had to be a member of The Council of Seven. Who else could wield this kind of raw power? He was about to tear Alex and I apart from the inside out, and there was nothing we could do about it. She crouched on the ground in much the same position I was, knelt on one knee, cradling her head in her hands as she looked up at Mr. Beelz. I wanted to lash out at him for hurting her, for making her kneel like that. I tried to find my feet, but the vibrating agony in my head redoubled, forcing my face to the sidewalk in excruciating supplication.

"As I said, Mr. Scott is under my protection, and I will not tolerate a threat to my charge."

That voice again, shrill and rat-like, cutting in like hot steel. It was almost worse than the torture.

"We really must be going; however, I look forward to learning about your involvement in Mr. Scott's affairs."

Mr. Beelz motioned toward a long, black blur. I assumed it was a limousine parked on the street, but the buzzing in my head made it impossible to make out. Simeon said something as well, but his words came out equally as muted. The only things that existed in my world was that audible, vibrating pain and Mr. Beelz's hammering voice.

Swirling, blurring colors mixed with a screeching buzz and threatened to drive me into a million white, hot needle points of madness. Then all at once, it was gone. Simeon ... Mr. Beelz. The sudden absence was so jarring, I fell the rest of the way to the ground as if someone had dropped me.

When I regained enough courage to open my eyes, I looked over to see Alex lying on the concrete as well. She wept into her palm, trying to get control of her sobs.

I crawled over to her, oblivious to the people walking past us on the sidewalk, and put a hand on her shoulder.

"You all right?"

Alex didn't look up at me, but she nodded her head. We both got to our feet and brushed ourselves off, trying to regain some semblance of dignity.

"Well, that was a sobering way to end an afternoon," Alex

said. "Next time we make drunk decisions together, let's make sure someone is there to slap it out of us before we follow through."

I laughed. The action brought lances of pain back into my head. "Next time we make drunk decisions together, you have my permission to slap me enough for both of us."

CHAPTER TWENTY-FOUR

The moment Alex and I stepped off the Envisage-nausea-elevator and back into The Nine, we were hit with hangovers so epic George Lucas would have been jealous. The penance was overkill measured by the megaton, making us both wish we could go back in time and make sure alcohol had never been invented.

I said goodbye to Alex and watched her stagger toward her apartment to sleep off her malady, but my sentence had just begun. I had screwed up big but allowing Judas to find out about my mistake from someone else would only make things worse. Like the kind of worse where you find yourself pantsless at that Llama castration clinic, and I don't mean the kind where the Llamas are castrated. Then again, it wasn't like I had gone up there to see Simeon. Running into him was an accident. Judas would understand. Maybe I didn't even need to tell him. It would blow over and everything— The Denarius in my pocket buzzed, and my stomach dropped like a lead bowling ball. Somehow, whenever Judas wanted to see me, he could page me through the coin. It was an irritating feature. I shoved my hand into my pocket as if to stifle the buzzing irritation.

There's no way he could know about Simeon. It had to be a coincidence ... didn't it?

I staggered off the elevator on the top floor of Judas's tower a few minutes later to see my favorite executive assistant waiting for me. She stood in front of her reception desk with her arms outstretched holding three little, white pills in one hand and a big glass of water in the other.

"How did you know ..."

She nodded toward the closing elevator doors.

"We have cameras mounted everywhere. This is not the first time I've seen an Agent wander in looking like they were on a six-week bender."

"We didn't even have that many." I popped the pills and drank the water, eternally grateful for both of the rare elements she offered. "I mean we had enough to get a little stupid, but this feels like we drank a gallon of gasoline with antifreeze chasers."

"Doesn't matter if you have one or one-hundred, when you return it's all the same. This place is supposed to be the ultimate punishment, remember? The establishment does not appreciate it when the residents go Topside for a good time. Sort of a reverse karma on steroids."

"Well, reverse karma sucks. Are there any other little idiosyncrasies about going Topside I should know about?"

"Loads." She rounded her desk and sat down in her chair again, turning her attention back to whatever task she had been doing before I came in. "It's way more fun if I let you find out on your own, though."

She looked up and shot me a wink. "Friendly tip, stay away from porn." She glanced down at my crotch and grimaced then looked up at me again.

"You can go on in. He is expecting you."

I stared at her for a moment wondering, then not wanting to wonder what that last bit of advice was meant to warn me against. I resisted shielding my nether regions with both my hands and smiled back at her.

"Thanks. For the tip and for the aspirin."

"Oh, aspirin doesn't work down here either. Hell, remember?"

I froze and jerked my head to look back at her. She acted like nothing had happened.

I waited while she read something impossibly interesting.

"Don't worry, they won't kill you." A hint of a smile touched her lips, but she refused to look back up at me. "But Mr. Iscariot might if you keep him waiting any longer."

I groaned and glanced back at the carved door that led to his office, knowing she was right. If she had poisoned me, it would be slower than a Judas homicide, but they would end the same either way.

I turned and headed for his office, head cradled in my hands, not bothering to knock or reach for the knob. As always, it swung open on its own, offering me entry to the sanctum of doom.

I did my best to straighten before rounding the corner and then shuffled forward to meet Judas's eyes. I was surprised to see he wasn't at his desk, but rather, he admired a new display on the far side of the room. His office was adorned with all types of paintings, tapestries, statues, and sculptures all portraying some sort of torture or tribulation. The sculpture he doted over now depicted a victorious soldier poised over a bloody battlefield. The soldier, however, seemed oblivious to the peasant who crouched behind him with a spear ready to stick him like a pig.

"What do you make of this capture in time?"

His eyes dropped from me back to the sculpture again. As gruesome as the battlefield rendering was, the piece looked incredibly intricate and lifelike. The fallen, both soldiers and peasants alike at his feet, looked to be made of real flesh, blood, and bone. The soldier wore a roman uniform, of course, his gladius held high in the air. The red fabric looked almost supple in the light. Behind him, the peasant assassin looked the most genuine of them all. I could read every line of determination on his face. Every bit of hate and sadness.

"The peasant has suffered and holds the soldier accountable," I said. "He wants to kill him for ..." I paused realizing how specific his reasoning felt to me.

"Kill him for what?" Judas prompted.

"He wants his life in exchange for his family. He wants the soldier to pay for destroying everything he loved and more."

Judas offered a thoughtful smile. "When I look at this piece, I see many things. A soldier doing his job. A peasant exacting retribution." He paused and placed a protective glass dome over the sculpture. "Perhaps the soldier was called to fight a band of murderous criminals, and he is the only survivor. Perhaps he fights for his country and has stood against the onslaught of countless invaders only to be cut down by a lowly traitor within his own ranks. The thanks he gets for his patriotism."

I was taken aback by the other scenarios, seeing the plausibility of every last one of them.

"I love this piece because it appears to be straight forward, but like life, there are so many sides to consider."

Judas turned and walked back to his desk where Procel and Mastema stood in their usual spots. I followed him over and sat down in the bone chair wondering, not for the first time, if they ever left their posts. I supposed Procel had come to fetch me in the past, but he came back as soon as he completed his task. No stopping off at the local Lucifer Mart for gum or a pack of cigarettes. Where did they go when Judas slept? Did they hover over his hammock like a couple of hungry vultures? Did they sleep themselves? All questions for another time. Maybe I could take Procel out for a Coke. Lord knows I didn't want any more bourbon.

"To what do I owe this pleasure?" Judas sank back in his chair and steepled his fingers the way he always did when he was thinking ... or expecting to choke me but didn't know why ... yet.

"But, you called me." Confusion kicked around the mass of paranoia already swirling in my brain. He must know now about Simeon. Or maybe he's waiting to see if I'd admit it. It was a test. Or maybe not. I had no idea what I should do.

I realized I was staring at Judas with my mouth half open, so I cleared my throat and sat back in my chair, trying to look casual.

"I mean, we can talk about whatever you want. Read any good books lately?"

I crossed my legs, uncrossed them, and then settled for clenching my hands onto the armrests as if it were an ejector seat about ready to go off.

Evidentially casual was not my strong suit today.

"I wanted to inquire about your freelance job. You seemed unsure about it last time you were here. Judging from your demeanor, I assume something has gone wrong."

I shouted out a laugh. "Of course not. What could go wrong? Everything is going right. So right it couldn't go any righter." I chucked a few more times but buckled under Judas's stony stare. "I guess I do have some other information you might be interested in."

Judas sighed and waved a hand by way of invitation.

I opened my mouth and thought for a minute, hoping something ... anything would come out.

"Jake Trento." I blurted so loud my voice cracked. "We ran into him Topside. He's been missing since that whole virus fiasco a few months ago."

I tried not to remind him how I had almost screwed up that

mission so bad that Jake and his partner had almost succeeded. I'm sure Judas remembered at any rate. He was like that.

"Jake said he's trying to figure out a way to stay Topside ... permanently. I'm not sure how, but he acted pretty hopeful about the whole thing."

Judas smiled. "He is not the first one to attempt such a thing, and he will not be the last. No one has ever discovered a way to circumvent the lasting effects of Topside Disease, and I doubt they ever will. It is beyond the understanding of the human world."

Judas eyed me and leaned forward in his chair. "Do not attempt to do this yourself. You will never outrun the disease, and its effects are eternal. The short victory you attain Topside will not be worth the eternal torture you endure afterward."

I shook my head remembering how certain pieces of Jake's anatomy fell off at random. "Don't worry. I have no desire to find out what it's like to come down with an atomic case of leprosy."

Judas dipped his head in agreement. "Is that all?"

I cringed knowing I needed to drop the bomb one way or another.

"Well ..." I tapped at my lip as if I were trying to remember any other details I had omitted. "We did a Topside recon of the train derailment; you'll be happy to know that horrible catastrophe is right on schedule. Puppies and children will be horrified."

I paused then raised my finger in the air. "Oh, I almost forgot. Probably not even worth mentioning. Alex and I got drunk and ran into Simeon. He had a guy with him. A gentleman named Robert Beelz. A little chatty but nice enough. Said he was with The Council."

I stood up and clapped my hands together ready to make my exit.

"That's about it. Have fun with your statues. I'll let you

know if anything way less boring happens, and I'll keep you posted about the whole train disaster."

Judas slammed his fists down on his desk, and his face turned so many shades of purple, I was pretty sure ultraviolet was one of them.

CHAPTER TWENTY-FIVE

J udas stood there for a moment like that, hunched over his
desk, hands pressed to the surface, as his brain built up
enough pressure to pop off like Mt. Vesuvius. I didn't move
either. Fear concreted my entire body, keeping me from scam-
pering like a scared, little guinea pig or sitting back down in the
chair.

The stalemate was broken when Judas picked up his heavy,
marble inkwell and hurled it across the room, shattering the
glass dome he had so carefully placed over the sculpture we
had admired just a few minutes earlier.

"Do you have any idea what sort of jeopardy you have put
this program in?"

I started to nod in agreement, but Judas held out a finger, all
but daring me to utter even a single word.

"I have operated the Denarii Division for thousands of
years and never has an Agent drawn the eye of The Council.
Not by accident and certainly not on purpose."

Judas screamed the last two words so loud spit came out of
his mouth, and the veins in his head pulsed with each syllable.

I wanted to say we hadn't run into Simeon and Mr. Beelz on

purpose, but it didn't matter. We had talked to them. We could've turned around and walked the other way. But we hadn't, and that was the problem. I started to make my plea anyway, but Judas's glaring eyes made me clamp my mouth shut so tightly my teeth clacked together.

"The Council of Seven is the most powerful entity in The Nine, next to the devil himself." Judas drove his fist into the desktop again. "And Mr. Beelz. Do you have any idea who that is? Does that name ring any bells for you? Robert Beelz? Bob Beelz? Beelz, Bob?

My face got tight with concentration, then fear and realization dawned. "Beelzebub."

It was a statement, not a question.

The right hand to Satan himself. Second in charge and the uppermost general. Prince of the underworld. Beelzebub could have destroyed Alex and I with a thought.

The Council of Seven seemed like a dangerous organization, but until now, it had been more like a foreign government. They could be intimidating but too far removed to worry about. I had just walked straight into the Nazi camp and invited Hitler over for matzah balls and gefilte fish. Judas was right. My arrogance had shoved me way past the line on this one.

"I'm sorry." It was all I could think to say. It wasn't enough.

"Sorry?" Judas paced out from behind his desk. He looked like he wanted to tear the walls down. He paused, glaring up at Procel. For a moment, I thought he might take his frustration out on the stoic Hellion, but apparently even Judas wasn't that insane.

Procel stood like a statue, never moving, but somehow even he wore the revolted expression of a persecutor. Mastema tracked me with her blindfold gaze as always, grinning her murderous grin. I had no idea which was worse.

"Operating with The Council's eye lurking over us will be all but impossible. Up till now, you have only managed to jeopardize your own missions, now you have jeopardized every mission, every Agent I have in the division."

I finally slumped back down in my chair, staring at the ground, not knowing what to say. Judas stood in silence for a moment as well, his back to me, face to the ceiling, then he sighed and raised a single finger.

"Mastema, if you please."

My eyes went up to the predatory looking demon crouched opposite him. Before I could react, her black leathery wings unfurled, and she pounced. Mastema was on top of me before I could even get out of my chair. She moved so fast it was inhuman. A streak of shadow rather than a proper assault. The talons on her feet hit me hard in the chest, knocking me backward over the chair, and she landed on top of me, perched on my body like a bird on a log.

I covered my face with my hands, expecting slashing blows from her sharpened claw fingers but none came. Instead she just stood there, crushing the air out of me with a grin on her face.

When she moved her arm, I jumped in spite of myself, but instead of tearing flesh from bone, she plucked the tiny lapel pin I wore off my shirt and tossed it to Judas.

With her task done, Mastema leaned down close to my face, sniffing at the air that surged out of my lungs. I tried to turn away, even throw her off, but she dug her taloned feet into my chest and held on like a bull-rider, forcing me flat every time I attempted to twist out from under her weight.

She caressed the side of my neck with a claw, then just as she began to dig in, Judas cleared his throat. "That will be enough."

Mastema let out a disappointed little coo then pushed off to glide back to her post behind Judas's desk again.

I laid there for a moment, trying to control my breathing,

and checked my neck and chest for claw shaped puncture wounds. When I didn't find any, I sat up and got to my feet.

Judas held the pin Mastema stole from me in his fingers. He displayed it in the air, teeth bared like an angry wolf. "Since you cannot rule your urge to get into mischief, I will keep this until I believe you are able to follow orders over emotion."

It was in that instant that I realized what he had stolen away from me. The tiny lapel pin looked unassuming enough. No one would think twice about it, but that pin meant everything to a Judas Agent. It was their passport to the Envisage Splice Transporter. Without that pin, the nausea elevator wouldn't work. I could no longer go Topside, at least not alone, and right now, that posed a huge problem.

"Please, you can't do that. I didn't mean to run into Beelzebub. It was just bad tim—"

"You wouldn't have run into him at all if you had followed my order to leave Simeon alone."

Judas was back to shouting again. This definitely wasn't going the right direction. I almost reminded him that Alex was with me so taking my pin away would only be half the punishment, but I managed to clamp my lips shut before my mouth dug a bigger hole for me to fall into. That didn't stop the panic I felt though. Without that pin, I couldn't go Topside alone. That meant I couldn't go up and prevent Alex's train from derailing in the town. I had to go Topside and sabotage the project, or a lot of people were going to die.

My mind raced for an answer. I couldn't plead with Judas to let me go. He was all pro-train crash. Smash and grab wasn't the answer either. The only thing getting smashed would be me.

Judas sealed my fate when he opened a small box on his desk, dropped the pin inside, and slammed the top shut. I heard the heavy, metallic click of a lock and knew it would take more than a set of nimble fingers to open it again.

"Get out of my office and pray that I do not decide to do more."

I stood up and started to make one last plea for my pin, but Judas cut me off.

"If you disobey orders again, I can assure you this pin will be the last thing you'll be worried about. Now get out."

I headed toward the door and thought about his words. How far would Judas go to punish me? How creative could he get with his punishments? The thought sent a chill up my spine. Had he ordered me to carry out Alex's train derailment or did he just say it was a good idea? As I walked out the door, I couldn't remember. Either way, the point was moot. If I didn't find a way to go Topside on my own, the derailment would happen according to Alex's plan, and there would be nothing I could do to stop it.

CHAPTER TWENTY-SIX

After my friendly chat with Judas, I wasn't quite ready to call it a night. It was still early, so I decided to hop on my wonder tricycle and pedal out to the shop to pay Zoe a visit.

I pumped my legs and realized I had more than a little energy left in the tank. Something that should have been long empty considering the brain mashing hangover I had had when I arrived at Judas's office. I felt great. More than great. I felt like I could ride to my shop and back a dozen times without breaking a sweat. I would have to ask what those special aspirins contained. Whatever it was, I wanted a case of them.

I sped through Scrapyard City in record time and found the shop windows and door open. Someone was home, although, whoever it was must have been in the back, checking stock.

I ambled up to the door and banged my fist on the outside of the wall. "Hey there, strangers. Anyone home?"

Zoe appeared from the back, tripping in as if she had sprinted through the door and realized she had to stop at the last second.

"Hello. Hi." She shot me a jerky wave. "What are you doing here? You never stop by this late. Is something wrong?"

I raised my eyebrows. "Wow, that's a lot of questions. I'm good. Just stopped by to see how you were doing. You look a little uptight. Is everything okay with you? Where are Jazzy and Meg?"

"I'm fine. Just checking the stock. They are out for a walk. You know, getting some air."

I screwed up my face in concern. "Two women out for an evening stroll in the picturesque streets of Scrapyard City? Are they trying to get kidnapped?"

Zoe rolled her eyes. "Stop trying to be our big brother. We can take care of ourselves."

I held up my hands in placation. "Just making an observation. Sue me for being concerned."

Zoe deflated a little and leaned against the door, looking a little more relaxed. "Sorry. I guess I'm a little sensitive. I didn't mean it. They'll be fine. They have the Blood Rakes hidden under their sleeves. If anyone gives them trouble, they'll be in for a big surprise."

Blood Rakes were a Hellion weapon we acquired when we had fought my cousins at the Skin Quarries several months ago. A hard-earned spoil of war and deadly gauntlet style hand to hand weapon. Zoe was right. Anyone messing with them would get a face full of unfriendly in a hurry, no matter who they were.

"So, what brings you by this late?" Zoe asked. "Don't tell me you were just in the neighborhood. I hear you scored an apartment in that fancy tower at The Judas Agency."

That stung a little. I hated to think of my friends sleeping out here in the wastes while I relaxed in safety. At least they had the shop. It had served me well for almost forty years. It would do the same for Zoe and her friends.

"Apartment might be a strong word. It's more of a human-sized drainage pipe, but it's comfortable." I looked around. "It doesn't have the character of this place though." I smiled at her and touched her arm. "How are you doing?"

"I'm good; business is good," she said. "You know, even though you're a big Judas Agent with your own fancy place, it doesn't mean you can't come hang out here."

"I will make a point to stop by more." I paused for a second. "I ran into a friend of yours. Marcus Trainer? The name ring a bell?"

Zoe tried to hide it, but I saw ever muscle fiber in her body stand on end. Her eyes would not come up to meet mine, and she began to fiddle with her fingers like a kid who had just been caught in a lie.

"It was an idea I had, but it didn't work out." I let the silence play out between us and then she continued. "To be honest, I thought a lot about our talk last time you were here, and you were right. All of these rescue missions are only risking the people I care about. It isn't helping anyone and saving those Disposables is going nowhere."

Zoe finally lifted her head and met my eyes. Hers were full of tears, and it broke my heart to see her that way. "I'm not going to do it anymore. I am through rescuing Disposables from the Skin Quarries. I'm not picking fights with The Wax Worx. My plans are here at the shop, helping where I can, when I can, with the Woebegone who survive around here."

I wanted to rejoice at her words, but I could see the turmoil warring within her. She wanted to save them all, but we were in The Nine. There was no way to rescue everyone. It was barely possible to save a few.

"I know this isn't what you wanted, but this shop is a way to help. It doesn't break people out of cages, but this place does give the Woebegone here something better. It gives them the power the take control of their existence. Part of it anyway. They can find something useful to do and earn a little piece of life in return. I know that doesn't seem like a lot, but it matters. I've seen more than one soul saved from the torment of the Sulfur Pools thanks to a simple Coke or a Twinkie. Don't knock it. You will change things through this rusty, old window. I promise."

Zoe nodded. "It would be nice to have you around here a little more. We miss you. Everyone does." Her eyes went down to the ground again. "Especially me."

Guilt twisted my insides into knotted, little shreds, and I found it difficult to look up at Zoe too. "I know. I haven't been around much. The Agency and projects at Hula Harry's have taken up all my time. I'll be back more though, I promise."

The silence between us was palpable. I let it hang for a second then broke in with a whiney voice.

"I don't even like the stupid apartment they gave me. It's small, too soft, impossible to climb into, and I have to sleep with a bunch of guys all packed in around me."

Zoe's eyes shot up along with her eyebrows.

"Well, not in the same bed. They're in different sleeping areas, but the thought of them being so close." I shivered.

Zoe let out a laugh. "I can see why you'd rather stay there than sleep in the shop with three beautiful women."

That stopped me. I had never even thought of it that way. What was I thinking? The bragging rights alone were enough to justify me staying at the shop.

"I have no argument whatsoever for that one."

Zoe laughed again.

"It's good to see you smile." I said offering her a smile of my own.

"You too."

I glanced in the direction of The Agency, already regretting the knowledge that I needed to get back. Zoe could see it in my eyes, and I felt ashamed that it even crossed my mind.

"Don't worry. I've got this place covered." Zoe offered me a smile so genuine it only served to twist the guilt dagger further.

"I know what this place means to you. Not the building or the stuff but what it stands for. It's a part of me too, and I'll never let that fall, I promise."

I nodded. "Thanks ... for everything. I know I saved you in the beginning, but lately, I feel like you're the one who's done all the saving. Thanks for looking out for me and the shop and even for looking out for the people you saved. You are a good person."

She rushed in and gave me a hug. "Thank you," she whispered. "I needed that." She held me tight before stepping back.

Thoughts of my historical search about her life entered my mind. I still couldn't believe Zoe was capable of doing something so heinous. I guessed we all had our crosses to bear. Mine was soaked in the misery of others too.

"I should get going if I want to be back before the monsters come out to play."

Zoe nodded. "Go on. Ride off into the sunset. But I'm holding you to your promise. I really do miss you."

I smiled. "I miss you too." I threw my leg over the trike and seated my foot on the pedal. "I'll be back before you know it." Then I pushed off, heading back the way I came.

CHAPTER TWENTY-SEVEN

I pedaled for about five minutes before I realized I had forgotten something. I usually left my Whip Crack at the shop in case the girls needed it for protection. Tomorrow, however, Alex and I were heading over to check out the place Marcus had told us about. If it turned out to be even one tenth the setup we thought it would be, Alex and I would need every weapon we could find.

I swung my wonder trike around and headed back to the shop to get it. I'd definitely have to hurry if I wanted to make it there and back before all the baddies came out to play. The last thing I needed was to be caught out riding a squeaky tricycle through the streets of Scrapyard City at night. It would be like announcing a free shooting gallery, except I was the only target ... and they were only allowed to use their teeth.

When I pulled up to the shop, I was surprised to see that Zoe had already buttoned everything up for the night. Meg and Jazzy must have shown up the second I had left, and they all decided to turn in. I couldn't help but remember Zoe's comment about sleeping with three beautiful women. It made me want to stay even more, despite the safety and comfort of

The Judas Agency apartments. There was something to be said about sleeping where you were free. The shop was mine ... ours and being cooped up in those agency comfort coffins felt a little too much like being in a cage.

I banged on the door to the shop as hard as I could. The place was all reinforced steel, so making noise from the outside was tough.

"Zoe, it's me. I forgot to get something. Let me in."

No answer. I grabbed a stray piece of metal off the ground and banged again.

"Zoe, it's Gabe. Let me in."

Still nothing.

I grunted with frustration and pulled the worn key out of my pocket.

"Ready or not, I am coming in, so you better cover up if you're prancing around in your skivvies."

I pushed the door open with one eye shut and the other half squinted. As my eyes adjusted to the dark, I realized no one was there.

"Nice. All that talk about the shop and watching out for the neighborhood and the second I leave, she bolts."

I shook my head and walked over to the secret panel located under the counter. I popped it open, and there sat my little beauty. At least Zoe hadn't taken the Whip Crack with her.

The moment I thought it, I felt guilty. Part of me would rather she had. Then she would have a weapon. The Blood Rakes were still missing. At least there was that. If I were a betting man, I would guess that Zoe had headed to wherever Meg and Jazzy were. They would be safe ... safer at least, together.

I grunted and yanked my Whip Crack out of its hidey hole and slammed the compartment shut again. If they wanted to run around risking their necks, that was their business. I had to quit worrying about them. Especially Zoe. She would do what she wanted and no amount of mother-henning would stop her.

I was about to walk out the door when my conscience caught me again. If she came back and found the Whip Crack gone, she might think someone had stolen it. She would wonder how they got in and might even go out looking for whoever took it. I couldn't let her do that. I should at least leave a note ... something to let her know I had it.

I peered around the inside of the shop looking for something to write on. Sticky notes weren't really a thing in The Nine, so I poked by head into the back to find some scrap ... anything. I climbed up the tall stairs and was surprised to discover more than our usual stock of Twinkies and Coke.

Lined up on the front seat and floor were several strange box-shaped electronics. Not the finished outer shells, but the raw metal skeletons and circuit boards. They all had a sort of clear, black orb on top and sported a trail of long wires out the bottom. It looked like Zoe— or someone else—had figured out how to hot-wire the things to a car battery as well. One of the shoebox sized contraptions had been rigged with clips capable of hooking to the fat terminals of one sitting next to it.

I leaned in close, examining the handy work. It didn't look complicated. The loose wires had obviously led to the previous power source to operate ... whatever these things did.

Zoe was up to her neck in something, and it didn't look good. I considered waiting her out. Sitting here in the shop until she got back and forcing her to explain what all these electronic doodads did. It wouldn't do any good. She would either tell me they were new snow cone machines or say she was holding some stuff for a friend. Either way, I doubted she would be honest with me. We were way past that. Even after our talk, it was clear she didn't care about this place. I began to wonder if she ever did. Whatever these things were, I would find out for myself, then come back and discuss it later.

I hefted one of the devices off the back of her pile and carried it out to the front of the shop. After a moment's hesitation, I decided a note was overkill too. Announcing I came back would only alert her to the fact that I saw her stash. At least the missing Whip Crack wouldn't be all that obvious.

I stomped outside, kicking the door shut, and slamming the lock home. The light was almost gone, so with my Whip Crack holstered over my shoulder, I tossed my new toy into the basket on the back of my trike and started pedaling. The anger that surged through my limbs made powering my ride much easier than normal. When would I learn not to trust people?

I pushed on through the dimming light consumed by my disappointment. I no longer cared whether it was dark or not. If any baddies jumped me from the shadows now, I'd say bring it on. I was in the mood for a fight.

CHAPTER TWENTY-EIGHT

Alex and I made our way to the warehouse Marcus had described. We were in a seedy part of town, like pretty much everywhere in The Nine. Shanty type buildings lined the maze of patchwork streets and pathways. Sheetmetal and spare steel lay strewn all over the ground, and Woebegone seemed to prowl and scurry like rats from place to place, searching for heat, food, security, anything not readily available to those who existed in The Nine.

"How much further is this place?" Alex walked with her arms at her sides looking like a gunslinger ready to draw. She wore her Song Reapers under the wide sleeves of her leather duster and was prepared to snap them out into action at a moment's notice.

I wore my Whip Crack holstered over the shoulder of a denim jacket. Hostility poured out of me, and if some lowlife wanted to feed my blades, I was happy to oblige.

"I have no idea. You heard Marcus same as I did. We get there when we get there."

"Wow." Alex peered back at me. "Did Godzilla pee in your cereal this morning?"

I huffed out a breath. "Sorry. I had a rough night. I went to the shop. Zoe and I had this long talk about taking care of the place and what really mattered. Turns out it was nothing but a big story to throw me off her scent."

Alex winced. "Sorry." She climbed over a tangled mess of wire, making sure to kept at least one of her arms free. "Zoe is her own breed. I'm not here to judge anyone's past, but it does speak to her character. All that information we found doesn't mean she's Scrapyard City's newest serial killer, but I think she's capable of a lot more than you're giving her credit for. She has a dark side. She's not the wholesome girl you knew when she was a brainless Freshborn. You need to accept that. She has baggage like the rest of us, and hers is full of a dark past. Like it or not, that's a part of her. Understand that, and you might not be happy, but you might find you are less disappointed."

I nodded. Lord knew I had my fair share of baggage. Far be it from me to expect anyone to drop theirs at the door.

"Thanks for the reality check. Sometimes I need a slap in the face to see straight."

"Anytime you want me to slap you, just say so. I'd be glad to do it right now." She raised a hand, and I grabbed her wrist to stop her. She had a Cheshire Cat grin on her face, but she didn't resist me.

"You're a good friend, but I'm okay for now. I'll let you know if anything changes."

Alex dropped her arm and shrugged. "Suit yourself. Maybe I'll surprise you later."

I chuckled, then pointed up ahead at a large structure; a place that big meant it was reinforced against firestorms somehow. That kind of integrity did not come cheap, which in turn meant corrupt, ruthless, and violent. All things I made it a policy to avoid ... pretty much never anymore.

"I think that's our spot."

Alex eyed the huge warehouse and let out a long whistle. "I

don't know who's in there, but that place is well funded. I don't know if we have the clout to kick in their doors."

"I feel like kicking anything in that place would earn us a whole lot of time in the Pools," I said.

"Marcus said the painting would be up near the dock in a red and yellow crate. How hard could it be to spot? Let's find a window to peek through."

Alex groaned. "Fine, but we're only looking. No Batman superhero entrances."

I laughed. "Come on. You can be Batgirl."

I started to slink forward, but Alex wrapped her fingers around my throat and squeezed.

"Call me that again, and I will slap you so hard you'll think you're the Batboy Wonder for real."

I held up a hand in surrender. "Okay, okay. Not Batgirl." I pulled away from her and made sure I was out of her reach then said, "How about Bat Lady or Bat Woman ... No wait ... Bat Broad."

Alex lunged for me, but I managed to stay just out of her reach. "And you can't say the Batboy Wonder. That's mixing up heroes. It's Batman *and* the Boy Wonder. You could pull that off with some yellow tights and a cape. All you would need is a cool mask. You already have the hair for it."

I took a step to run and avoid Alex's wrath when a lower level Hellion showed his tall, lanky form outside one of the warehouse doors. Alex and I both dove for a stack of crates to conceal our location next to the wall.

I peeked through a crack between the boxes, trying to spot the Hellion, when pain accosted my right ear. I stifled a scream as Alex all but twisted my earlobe off and pulled me back toward her.

"I am going to twist this thing until you look like an elf if you don't take back everything you said."

She twisted harder, and I winced, tilting my head to try and minimize her leverage.

"I take it back." I shout-whispered. "I take it all back, everything I've ever said. Everything about you, about bats, about girls, everything."

"And Bat Broad?" She twisted harder.

"Terrible idea. Who would even think of something that sexist? I wouldn't want to be associated with someone like that."

Alex let go, and I sank six inches to the ground.

"I'm so glad we have these little chats." Alex shoved me to the side and peeked through the crack I had been looking through.

I pulled myself back up. "What's with you trying to twist off my ears lately?"

"What's with you saying things to deserve it?"

She had a point.

"The Hellion's gone. Peek through that window and tell me what you see."

She pointed up to a dirty pane of glass above us. I would have to stand on one of the crates to peer inside, but the window should give me a clear-ish view of the dock area without exposing us too much.

"Okay. Tell me if our friend comes back."

"Any more cracks, and I will call him over and throw you into his arms."

"Sheesh," I whispered. "You really have a thing for bats."

Alex turned to glare at me, but I ignored her and climbed up to peek through the window.

"What do you see?"

I groaned. "Well, the good news is I see the crate. It's a ways back in the warehouse, but it's on a table right out in the open."

"What's the bad news?"

I ducked back down behind the boxes and crouched next to

Alex. "It's surrounded by about a half-dozen low-level Hellions and a bunch of Woebegone thugs. That place makes the mafia look like a bunch of preschool teachers."

"One Hellion was bad enough," Alex said. "We can't stand up to six of them and a bunch of Woebegone. There's only so far I'm willing to go for a Coke."

I looked around, trying to think, when I noticed something across the way. Something no Hellion gangster would leave home without. A rusty Cadillac complete with smoked out windows and chrome rims.

"I have an idea."

CHAPTER TWENTY-NINE

I stood on the crate below the window, watching the Hellions and Woebegone inside the warehouse. There seemed to be two separate groups. One belonged to the warehouse itself and was comprised largely of the Woebegone staff. They worked at pulling or rearranging the warehouse stock while a single Hellion supervisor orchestrated the whole thing. He wasn't huge by demon standards but compared to a human-sized Woebegone, he was Conan the Barbarian with Rocky Balboa riding on his shoulders.

He had an insectoid look to him: greenish with an exoskeleton and long, mantis-style arms. He looked like he could swing one of those limbs out like a machete and hack half the staff in two if he wanted.

The rest of the occupants looked to be a visiting set of Hellions of all shapes and sizes. Some squat and heavy, some tall and lean. They were all of the lower level variety, like Bug Face, but just as deadly when it came to the tender anatomy of a Woebegone. They seemed to be negotiating the sale of a few items, one of which was the three-foot red and yellow crate I was interested in. The flat box sat on a table with several other antiquities, and Bug Face was deep in negotiations with a squat demon so wide he had to waddle from foot to foot in order to move.

I watched them haggle and barter. At one point, the negotiations reached a fever pitch, but, in the end, they shook hands ... pincers, whatever, and several of the demons behind Squatty began gathering up the loot to leave.

I backed off my perch to scan the street. Alex should have pulled off her little stunt by now, and I began to worry that she ran into some trouble of her own. Before I could abandon Plan A and dive headlong into B, the Cadillac parked outside the warehouse roared to life.

Fit for a funeral, this stretched-out luxury job billowed smoke and unholy noise from every orifice. The engine roared a few more times, then the rear tires howled out a scream of rubber, and the demon-mobile tore off down the street, dodging debris and gaining ground with every second.

The warehouse docks spewed low level demons like a shotgun blast with them hurling down the street at full speed. Even Squatty was along for the ride in what looked like a baby carrier on steroids attached to a much beefier Hellion with long legs. One of the Hellions sprouted wings and took flight. That wasn't something we had planned for. I hoped Alex could hold them off long enough for me to snatch the goods and make my getaway. An airborne pursuer might be a game changer on her end.

There was nothing I could do about it now. Alex had done her job. Now I needed to do mine.

I climbed onto the crate again and peeked into the warehouse. Just as had I hoped. Nothing but Woebegone personnel left to tend to the stock. Time to go to work.

I unholstered my Whip Crack, and the rasp of blades announced my arrival at the open bay door. The workers inside took one look at me standing there, seething for blood with my hungry weapon, and ran the other direction. I didn't know where the other exits were, but they abandoned the place like rats on a sinking ship. Not one of them stood their ground.

Don't get me wrong. Part of me was overjoyed that I didn't have to fight my way into the warehouse, but not even one? I expected more from a staff employed by a Hellion crew boss.

I shrugged and hurried over to the table where the crate rested, still stacked along with the other antiquities Squatty and his buddies had bartered for. There were works of art, statues, and even a vase that looked to be Egyptian or maybe Roman in origin. I didn't see what they had paid, but it must have been a bundle. These things were old and that equaled expensive no matter where you were.

I ignored the more impressive pieces exposed on the table and focused on the painting. I set my Whip Crack on the ground at my feet then reached for a crowbar placed next to the crate. Maybe it was part of the convenience package. After a bit of prying and well-placed effort, the front of the crate popped free. I lifted it away to reveal the contents and was aghast to see the most horrifying clown painting I have ever witnessed in my life. This guy would clear out the circus and scare away every lion, tiger, and monkey in the big top.

The clown wore a painted blue smile that read pure child-molesting mass-murderer. His hair was a shock of greasy red covered by a decayed bowler hat. He had a cracked red nose which bore a spider from its nostril and an oversized bowtie that had been pulled and jerked to the point of near failure. Almost as if someone else had used it as a handhold in a last-ditch effort to ward him off and failed. The paint was cracked, and the finish dulled by time. If there were a more horrifying image put to canvas, it would be registered as a terrorist weapon.

I slammed the lid back on the crate and realized I had been holding my breath. I gasped in a long pull of air then let it out again. I didn't know how Dan got mixed up with this clown-loving Hellion, but if this painting was any indication as to his demeanor, squirting flowers and rubber chickens were definitely not his bag. We needed to do this deal and get Dan in the clear, or I had a feeling losing his bar might be the least of his worries.

I tapped a couple of the nails back into the top, holding the crate together, more for my sake than the painting's, then went to pick it up. Before I could, the dock door rumbled to life with a jaw rattling creak and began to go down. Out of instinct, I reached over my shoulder for my Whip Crack, but as soon as my hand hit the empty holster, I realized my mistake. It was at my feet on the floor. I dove for it, already knowing I was too late. Just as I thought, my hand found nothing but bare concrete and dust. My weapon had been swept away by a sickly green carapace. Bug Face had hung back to meet me after all.

CHAPTER THIRTY

"I don't suppose we could talk about this." I spied my Whip Crack behind Bug Face on the ground. He had reached in with his other foot and swept it out of reach. "Would you believe I'm an art lover?"

Bug Face emitted a series of mucousy clicks and clacks. His mandibles flexed like a worker ant's when he spoke, making it look more like he was licking his chops than trying to communicate.

"Sorry, I don't speak bug." I managed to work my way around, so the table stood between the two of us, affording me at least some sort of shield. "Why don't we circle back when you pupate lips?"

Bug Face lashed out with his mantis-style arm, slashing it through the air so fast I wound up back on the floor trying to dodge it. He followed up with a downward chop that cleaved the one-inch solid steel tabletop in half. The noise sounded like a thousand kindergarteners grating their chairs across the floor at the same time. It was deafening. The two halves crashed to the ground, and the weight of the table made the Earth vibrate beneath me. Stunned by Bug Face's power, I almost forgot to duck out of the way of his next slash.

I managed to dodge a sweeping crosswise strike, but the shelf next to me wasn't so lucky. His mantis machete cut the legs out in one fell swoop. The noise didn't sound nearly as impressive this time, but Bug Face would pay a higher price for his careless swing.

I rolled and kept on rolling as I saw what was about to happen. The shelf Bug Face cut was tall and heavy. It reached almost all the way to the two-story ceiling, and it was filled with antiquities that were priceless both Topside and in The Nine.

The shelf toppled like a tree in the forest. Slowly at first, then it gained speed. Crates, pottery, and busts all slid from the safety of their shelves and crashed to the ground. I watched as Bug Face realized his mistake. He attempted to use his strength to keep the shelf from falling. Too bad he didn't possess those two little things called opposable thumbs. They couldn't slash through a table, but they were handy when you wanted to save an inventory of priceless art.

The shelves slid across the slick shell of Bug Face's segmented arm and kept on falling. When the heavy mass hit the shelves next to it, they began to topple like over-sized dominoes as well. By the time I was through to the other end of the row, I watched one shelving unit after another crash to the ground in thundering rounds of dust, ancient pottery, and glass. The storm of destruction did not diminish until the last unit was down.

I crouched there for a moment, ready to run, dodge, or fight. The dust and silence hung in the room like a heavy fog until a guttural shriek sliced through it from the other side. It sounded like a Pterodactyl on the hunt for its favorite meal, and Gabe Fricassee was at the top of the menu.

Who was I kidding? I couldn't fight that thing. My only hope was to hide or outrun him. Hiding wouldn't work, since

Bug Face probably knew every inch of his vast warehouse. That left running … through a disaster of fallen debris and dust so thick I could spoon it like soup.

A noise began to approach through the settling cloud. Something like Babe Ruth beating his way through a forest of old, metal trash cans with a baseball bat. Bug Face growled out clicks and clacks of what had to be profanity and fury. Whatever he said, I had a feeling it wasn't a concern for my safety.

I turned and scampered further into the building. There had to be a way out of this mess. The Woebegone workers had abandoned the place faster than cockroaches in an apartment fire. There must be a way for me to escape.

I waved a hand in front of my face and fought to keep myself from coughing. After a couple of seconds, I came to a wall, then a door. I jerked it open and dove inside, slamming the door shut behind me. Good news—the air was clear and breathable. Bad news—it was only a room. The door hadn't led outside the way I'd hoped.

The place looked like some sort of break area for the Woebegone workers in the warehouse. It contained a few lockers and tables, but no chairs. The vending machines held nothing but crusty meal replacement bars and a countdown timer on the wall began to click down from ten minutes as soon as I walked through the door. Worst break room ever.

Bug Face inched closer with every moment, and there was no other way out. The sound of tearing metal and shattered glass unnerved me even more than the countdown timer. I had no other choice. I would have to stand and fight, but without my Whip Crack, I wouldn't have much of a chance. I hurried over to the lockers and started jerking them open one by one, hoping to find an item to use as a makeshift weapon. A pipe, an old wrench, maybe a bazooka. In the fifth locker, I hit pay dirt. I couldn't help but laugh. Seemed the local union had a walkout planned. I could hardly blame them, considering the contents of those vending machines. Not even one bag of Fritos.

I grabbed the large, plastic bottle. It was about the size of your average household cleaner, minus the spray nozzle. Too bad. The ability to squirt this stuff would be better than a bazooka.

I twisted off the lid and waited by the door, poised to launch my chemical warfare objective.

The tearing and breaking got louder then paused. Bug Face had finally dug his way through the carnage to my side of the warehouse. Now he was trying to figure out where I had gone. It only took about six seconds before one of his mantis-style cleavers cut the door in half, and a sickly, green limb kicked the rest of it out of the way, leaving room for Bug Face to come inside.

I held my ground, crouched just to the side of the door. As soon as Bug Face showed his ugly green mug, I let him have it.

I squeezed the bottle of DEET, and threw it at his face, splashing the wet chemical all over his head. Bug Face reared back, trying desperately to wipe the oily compound away. It wouldn't kill him, but to Bug Face, DEET was pretty much like getting maced, tear gassed, and pepper-sprayed all at the same time. He wouldn't be happy, but I hoped to buy myself enough time to sneak past him and out of his warehouse.

I ran toward the front of the building. Bug Face had cut quite a swath in his fury to get at me. I barely had to duck or dodge any debris at all. Once I was past the wreckage, I saw the bisected table with the painting and my Whip Crack nearby. To my surprise, so was Alex. She stood just inside an exit, next to the big rolling door that Bug Face closed to trap me inside.

"What did you do?" Alex's face was a mask of fear and astonishment. "I thought they were going to be pissed about the car, but this..."

I holstered my Whip Crack, grabbed the crate containing the painting, then sprinted toward the door.

"Yeah, well, one of them is still here, and he's an armored tank of slashy anger. Let's get out of here before he introduces himself."

Alex held the door for me so I could squeeze though with my bulky payload. "Have any trouble with your party goers? I was worried when I saw one of them had wings."

"We can trade war stories later." Alex followed me out and slammed the door, eyeing the roadway, then the sky behind us. "For now, let's get this thing back to Hula Harry's. The longer we're out in the open, the more likely we'll pick up a tail."

I agreed with a nod and started off in a jog.

Alex followed suit, keeping her head on a swivel while I concentrated on not falling on my face.

"Remind me to stop helping you with these little adventures," Alex grumbled. "I like my face where it is. I'm tired of your angry friends trying to tear it off."

I chuckled. "Think of all the fun you'd miss. When was the last time you got to drive a Cadillac in Hell?"

Alex huffed. "Cadillacs are fine. I just don't like all the suicidal complications."

I hopped over a bent piece of rusted angle iron and smiled. "Picky, picky. Next you'll want a wet bar too."

"More running and less talking. This isn't the only job we have to do today, and I'd like to be in one piece when we get to the next one."

CHAPTER THIRTY-ONE

I shook off the remnants of another spectacular dumpster landing outside the rail yard near the Oregon Sea Port. I had all but given up the thought of using the Envisage Splice with any dignity. If there was a dumpster, a cesspool, or even a poodle sized pile of dog doo, I would land in it. Presently, my boots marinated in the remnants of a ranch dressing soaked salad that had baked in the sun too long. At least it was better than poop ... barely.

"Don't you think we've had enough excitement for one day?" I scraped my boot in the gravel to remove the remains of my unwanted roughage. "Why are we back in another train yard?"

"Relax," Alex said. "Unlike your missions, this one is well-planned and does not involve scores of Hellion guards or stealing cars on the fly."

I scoffed. "I wouldn't say there were scores of Hellion guards. A bunch, maybe even a horde, but definitely not scores."

I looked up from my foot scraping to see Alex eyeing me with that *I'm about to do something painful to your body* look.

"Or scores are good. We can go with scores."

Alex looked away and kept walking. "I just want to be sure our train is on time. It should be pulling out this afternoon. I don't want anything going wrong with this operation."

"What could go wrong?" I said almost under my breath. "We're going to crash a train right in the middle of a city and kill hundreds of people. Seems like a bullet proof party to me."

This time Alex did turn around to face me. "I am getting a little sick of reminding you of why we're doing this." She paused. "Actually, I don't know why I keep using the word 'we.' You haven't done anything but complain since I came up with this idea. It would've been nice if you had lifted a pinky to help, but I didn't even ask for that. I'm trying to secure both our positions in The Agency. The least you could do is be a little grateful for it."

I wanted to say something helpful, but I couldn't even make myself look her in the eye. Bottom line, Alex had decided to willingly kill lots of people, and I was not okay with that, no matter what it did for our reputation at The Agency or my cover and credibility in the Denarii Division. I had to stop her, and if not her, then I had to stop the train. And since Judas grounded me by taking away my Splice pin, I had no idea how I would do either.

When I didn't meet Alex's gaze, she snarled out an angry groan and kept walking.

"This is our train. Try not to screw anything up while I'm gone. I have a contact in the dispatcher's office. I'm going to find out if anything's been delayed. You stay here and pout or whatever it is you've decided to do on this job."

Alex stormed off toward the main building in the yard while I hung back, trying to make myself invisible. I watched as crews checked the open cars and the locomotives set to pull them. They worked the train back and forth, adding the last of the hoppers, all empty coal carriers, and a few box cars on the end. Nothing remarkable. Nothing to sabotage from here either, at least not in a way that would stop the trip from happening. I stayed to the shadows, watching helplessly as Alex's mile long battering ram built itself and got ready to leave. The actions of the yard staff looked so innocuous. They had no idea they were loading the shell into a cannon.

I watched as the rail workers operated like a well-built machine, everyone doing their part ... all but one man standing next to the end of the line. Better dressed than the rest of the yard crew, in jeans, a polo, and nice coat, he seemed to loiter, glancing up and down the line. No one expected him to work or give orders. He was just a part of the landscape, yet there for a reason. The whole scenario felt familiar somehow, but I couldn't lay my finger on why.

Before I could figure it out, Alex came jogging toward me looking almost giddy. "Everything's on track." She snorted. "No pun intended."

She turned her gaze toward the train, her grin unwavering. "This is actually going to work. I can't believe it." She grabbed my arm and shook it like she had just been called down as the next contestant on The Price is Right. She was so excited, she even danced a little, hopping jig. It about made me sick.

How could she be so excited about killing innocent people? Alex—the partner I had come to know and trust. The woman I would have laid my life down for, but now ...

I managed to paste on a plastic smile and went in for a congratulatory hug. The moment I threw my arms around her, Alex stopped dancing. For a second, she did nothing, but then she hugged me back. It was about as awkward a moment as awkward got, but I pushed through and then stepped away from her.

"Thanks for doing all of this. I know I haven't been all that grateful."

Alex eyed me with suspicion. "Not that I don't appreciate the sudden gratitude, but why the change of heart?"

I shrugged. "I had a moment to think while I watched these people work the train. Everyone's life is temporary right? Why am I getting so hung up on rushing a few of them to their final destination? This is going to be great for our careers. We can make it up to them later. Maybe Dan can give them free Cokes, at least the ones that end up in The Nine." I laughed, feeling sick to my stomach. "Really, thanks for setting this up. You can count on me to have your back from now on."

Alex still didn't look all that convinced, but her infectious smile would not be stamped out by my B-movie acting or anything else.

"All right then." Alex grabbed hold of my arm, reestablishing our physical connection. I couldn't help but feel the familiar jolt of electricity at her touch, although, now it felt tainted and sickly. "Let's head back home to celebrate. All we need to do now is wait until the train hits the last waystation before Bozeman. We'll meet it there, force the engineer to get it rolling, then kick everyone off, and watch the fireworks."

I nodded. "Like I said, sounds pretty bulletproof."

I smiled, turning my attention forward as we walked out of the yard, feeling the familiar shape of a metallic lapel pin hidden in my hand.

CHAPTER THIRTY-TWO

Getting back to The Judas Agency without Alex noticing her missing lapel pin had been easy. As long as we were together, the jump back went like it always had. Returning the pin before she noticed it was gone would be a different story. In the meantime, my newfound computer skills came in handy for finding the right location for my little sabotage operation. Skills might be a strong word. There was a considerable amount of cursing, shouting, punching, and even a few creative threats involving the program's circuitry that I was not proud of. All in all, it brought me to the place where I now stood. The Strough's Bridge over Trestle Creek. It was a ragged gouge in the Earth deep enough to hide a high-rise building and twice as wide. The bridge was an all metal marvel of I-beams, cables, and steel plates. A behemoth of modern engineering, and I needed to bring it all down.

I climbed over the guardrail about a quarter way down and tried not to think about what the fall would do to my body if I slipped off the slick under-framing. It was almost dark, making it harder to see, but the rocky bottom was still there. I would heal, in theory, but that almost made it worse. Surviving a fall meant I would feel every bone-breaking, organ-exploding moment of impact. A sensation I had no desire to experience.

The beams underneath the bridge were massive. Much larger than they seemed in the photos. My evil computer showed me which ones to compromise, but even with the right intel, this would take a while. Not good. Every moment I had Alex's pin in my possession sunk me in the circumstantial evidence department. She would either think I stole it to get here because I didn't have mine, true, or think I stole it to keep her from following me. Not true, but I probably would have if the first part weren't necessary.

Nothing to do about it now. I was here. Time to go to work.

I tried to make myself comfortable in a crook of the support structure and laid my hands on either side of one of the beams. My Topside power was pretty lame as superpowers went. I could rust out metal with my hands. Not as cool as Alex's fire power, but I had been practicing. At first, I could only manage a little hand shaped surface rust, but after a while, I was able to rust through sheet metal with a fair amount of effort. I had no idea how long it would take to rust all the way through these heavy support beams. Considering they were designed to carry tons of cargo, I definitely had my work cut out for me.

BNSF was the only railroad who used this line, and our train was the next one scheduled to make the trip across. I just had to be sure the bridge failed when it arrived. If all went well, it would be a wild west style train crash into the ravine. No people to hurt, no buildings to destroy, no rivers to pollute. Just a small creek and a whole lot of steel and coal dust. It should be a spectacular show.

I sat there concentrating all my effort into my hands, feeling the metal beneath my palms begin to bubble and flake. It went from smooth and weathered to fat and brittle. It would take a lot more time to wear all the way through, and I needed to rust through more than one, but this would work.

Evening came and went as a full moon took the place of the twilight glow, allowing me to see the remaining girders I needed to rust before I left for the night. My mind raced as I sat there, swirling with thoughts of Alex. I wanted to believe deep down that ambition had blinded her. She was a good person; I had to believe that. But having a position at The Judas Agency meant safety and security. A place to live and belong. A situation very few Niners got to enjoy. It was too much for Alex to gamble against.

The hug at the train station haunted me too. It was not a passionate kiss or a profession of true love, but Alex had taken it for more than it was—a veiled ploy to steal her lapel pin. Worse than that, I wanted to feel it too. I wanted to believe there was something between us, but this whole train idea had my head screwed on sideways. What if she wasn't the woman I thought she was? What if The Agency really had turned her heart cold? I could never be with someone like that ... could I?

A noise brought me out of my ruminations, and I lifted my head to the tracks above me. It wasn't possible, yet there it was. The unmistakable click-clack of an oncoming train. I stopped pouring power into the last beam and turned my ear to the sky. It came from the West. The wrong direction. A locomotive headed that way would run headlong into our coal train way before it got to my bridge disaster. That was unless the other train triggered the collapse first.

I scrambled out of my perch, no longer worrying about the long trip to the rocks below. If I fell now, it would be a blessing compared to being tangled in a mass of screaming steel and locomotive parts.

As I clambered up off the rusted bits of metal, the bridge groaned and creaked under its own weight. Suddenly, I worried that I had taken away too much of its stability. If it collapsed before the train got here, all would be lost as well. Maybe Alex was right. I didn't think my plans through all that well. I had become so focused on rusting out the bridge and seeing a crash that I never considered any other logistics.

The clacking got louder as I made it onto the top of the bridge. I started running as soon as my feet hit the railroad ties. Flagging the train down crossed my mind, but even if I got the engineer's attention, they would never be able to stop in time. Plus, how would I explain that I knew the bridge was unstable? No. I just had to get out of the way, hide, and watch the consolation show. I was just about to hide in a nearby stand of brush when another thought hit me. There would be a conductor, and an engineer, and maybe passengers on that train. What if I had sabotaged a passenger train full of people, thereby causing a disaster even bigger than the one I wanted to prevent?

I ran faster. My heart and thoughts raced. Images of passenger cars filled with screaming people plummeting to the rocky depths below filled my head. Chance or no chance, I had to try and stop that train from reaching the bridge.

Lights came into view around the bend. I started waving my arms like a wild man as I ran, but something didn't seem right. The lights were too dim, too low to the ground, and there were two of them. Didn't trains only have one big light in the middle?

I slowed to a jog and watched as the lights got closer. It wasn't a train at all. It was … a truck, on the railroad tracks. It took a moment for my brain to rectify the dichotomy. A maintenance truck running the line. And if the driver saw me …

I dove behind a bush and prayed I hadn't been noticed. The truck approached, click-clacking along the line, louder and louder, then it passed by without slowing down, heading straight for the bridge.

I simultaneously stood up, crouched back down, opened my mouth to shout, and shut it again several times. What if the bridge failed under the truck's weight? What if it didn't? Did I stop the truck and save the driver's life or let him go and hope the bridge held until the locomotive came to trigger the collapse as planned?

I held my breath as the decision was made for me. The truck made it to the bridge and kept on going. About a quarter the way down, I saw brake lights. The same spot I had sat for the past few hours doing my work. The truck slowed almost to a stop, then the brake lights went off, and the truck continued, never wavering again.

As soon as the truck rolled back onto solid ground again, my breath came out in a whoosh, and I collapsed to the dirt. If there were any more trains, trucks, or hand pumped carts scheduled to cross that bridge, I hoped it wasn't until after our locomotive arrived the next afternoon.

I couldn't worry about it anymore. I had to get back. It was late, and I promised to meet Alex at Hula Harry's so we could present Dan with the painting we retrieved. He hadn't been there earlier, so we hid it in his storeroom. After all the trouble we went through to get it, we both wanted to see his face when we gave it back to him. I hurried through the darkness, using the moon as my lantern, and hoped Alex hadn't noticed her missing pin while I was gone.

CHAPTER THIRTY-THREE

By the time I got the Hula Harry's, I was too exhausted to blink. Between our rumble with the demons in the morning, the trip to the railway in the afternoon, and then working on the bridge for the last few hours in the evening, I was stretched about as thin as a paper mattress. I didn't want to deal with Alex, Dan, the painting, or anything else. I didn't even want to stand. I just wanted to get this night over with so I could find the nearest soft spot and collapse onto it.

"Where have you been?"

I bit back a curt answer to Alex's greeting and offered a smile instead.

"Just working some bugs out at the shop." I lied, hoping she hadn't checked there before coming to the bar. "Sorry I'm a little late. The bugs were a little more persistent than I thought."

"They must have been filthy too. You haven't even changed out of your Topside gear. You look like you've been rolling around in a rusty barrel."

I glanced down at my coat and pants and realized that I had

not only neglected to change, I even forgot to brush off the evidence of my betrayal.

"Yeah." I made a show of sweeping off the metallic dust with my hands. "I had to dig into the foundation under the shop. That last firestorm really did a number on the place."

Alex stared at me while I tried to clean myself up then grabbed my wrist. "All right, you are just making it worse. Hold still."

The aggressive manner in which she began to swipe at my coat and pants seemed more like an assault than assistance. I endured the open-handed slap-brushing as long as I could—about five seconds—then I pushed her away, trying to defend against the onslaught.

"Okay, that's enough. Thank you very much." I took a couple of hops backward for good measure. "Your help seems a little more ... enthusiastic than usual. Something wrong?"

Her hand went straight to where she usually wore her lapel pin. Snap. She knew. I opened my mouth to try some sort of cover story, but Alex beat me to it.

"I lost my lapel pin somehow." She slumped back onto her stool and faced the bar again, looking more than a little distraught. "I can't believe I did something that stupid."

I winced and sat down next to her. "Relax, I'm sure it happens all the—"

"No, it does not happen all the time," she snapped back at me. "Losing a lapel pin is no small thing. I have no idea what they'll do to me."

I huffed out a laugh and regretted it the second the sound passed my lips. Alex shot me a sideways glare and then shook her head. "I wouldn't expect you to understand."

"Whoa." I leaned back on my stool. "Just because I play things a little loose doesn't mean I'm irresponsible."

Alex eyed me without saying a word.

"Okay, I might be a little irresponsible, but that doesn't

mean I don't understand the definition of responsibility. I owned a dictionary ... once."

That drew a chuckle from Alex, and she turned her gaze back to the rows of useless alcohol lining the wall again. When she didn't say anything, I unfastened *her* lapel pin from my collar and slid it to her across the bar.

As soon as she saw it, her head jerked back in my direction. "You can't do that."

I was about to tell her the truth when she shoved it back to me again.

"You can't give me your pin," she stammered. "I mean, that may be the nicest thing anyone has ever done for me but ..."

Her eyes went up to mine, and the words poised to come out of my mouth retreated back down my throat.

We stared at each other like that for a moment, then I laid my hand over hers and pushed the pin back to her again. "Keep it. It's yours. Don't worry about me. I get in trouble all the time. Sabnack will expect me to lose my pin. It'll be less of a shock."

The lie of omission tasted bitter, but the look of admiration in Alex's eyes made it all worth it. Of course, if she ever found out I had stolen that pin in the first place, that amorous expression would turn to murder in a hurry. I decided to live in the moment.

Alex peered down at our hands and then back up at me again. "Thank you. You know, sometimes you surprise me."

I smiled back at her. "Don't worry. I'll make sure the next surprise is a bad one."

Alex giggled and stood up from her stool, leaning toward me. "Sometimes bad can be good." She winked at me.

My heart, pretty much my whole body, jumped into overdrive. In that moment, I didn't care that she was the kind of person who could plan to ram a train into a town. All I wanted to do was to pull her close to me. I squeezed her hand. She smiled and took a breath as she leaned closer. Her lavender honey scent all but overwhelmed my senses. "Maybe I can show you how good bad can be."

I leaned forward ever so slightly, matching her move ... then Dan walked up and ruined the whole thing.

"So how did it go this morning? I am dying to hear. Alex wouldn't say anything until you showed up."

We both turned to face him. Alex was so close I could feel the warmth radiating from her body. Our dual stares were enough to make him fade back a step.

"What?" Dan raised an eyebrow. "What did I say?"

Alex sighed and backed away from me, and I resisted an urge to throw a glass at Dan's head. I held onto Alex's hand, letting it linger there for a moment before I reluctantly let go.

"Come on. Let's give it to him before he has a stroke." Alex walked away, heading for the storeroom.

"I may have a stroke." I let the simple statement hang, and Alex laughed. But I followed her back, trailed close behind by Dan and his ever-present dish towel.

When we got there, I made sure no one inside the bar could see us hit the panel leading to Dan's secret room and opened it up. There wasn't much space, but we had concealed the thin crate behind a stack of soda cases. When I pulled it out, Dan beamed with excitement.

"I can't believe you got this back." He threw the dish towel over his shoulder and took the crate in his hands. "Did you check it out?"

I nodded. "Sort of wish I hadn't. That thing is horrifying."

Alex scoffed as Dan set the crate against the wall and worked the top free. When she got a look at the horror show for herself, she recoiled.

"Whoa, who would want something like that? The only thing that painting's good for is years of therapy."

Dan nodded. "That's what this Hellion likes. The creepier the better. He put in a special request for this one."

"If he has something creepier than this monstrosity, I don't ever want to see it." I shivered.

Dan fastened the top back onto the crate and beamed at the both of us. "I don't know how I can ever repay you, but I swear, someday, I will."

"Let's stick to the free drinks for now." I winked. "We can discuss terms on indentured servitude later."

"Gastrith said he would send one of his minions to the drop spot tonight. I need to run if I am going to make it in time. I hate to ask one more favor, but how would you two feel about closing the place up for me? Everyone's pretty much gone. All you have to do is lock the doors on your way out."

"Free reign in a bar? That's like one of my all-time bucket list dreams," I exclaimed.

"Too bad you already kicked the bucket." Alex chuckled. "Go ahead. We'll get the place buttoned up for you. Don't worry."

Dan smiled again. "Who knew Judas Agents were so nice?"

"Don't tell anyone," I shouted as he walked out the door. "Or Alex will have to live up to her reputation."

CHAPTER THIRTY-FOUR

We watched Dan walk out the door, then I turned to Alex and winked. "Dad's gone, and we have the whole place to ourselves. Whatever shall we do?"

Alex shot me a sly grin then walked back over to her usual stool and sat down. "I'd say we should raid the liquor cabinet, but that won't do any good. Besides, last time we had a drink together, I swore I would never touch the stuff again."

I remembered the atomic fusion hangover from our little Topside indulgence. I swore the same thing; although, I still needed to find out about the magic white pills I had gotten in Judas's office.

"I say we give these nice folks another half an hour, then show them the road." Alex reached over the bar and cracked open a fresh can of Coke. "I don't want to be wandering the streets too late."

I scoffed. "Alex Neveu, the big, bad Judas Agent, scared of the dark." I poked her shoulder. "Who would have guessed?"

Alex gave me a dangerous look and sipped her Coke. "Things in the dark are scared of me. I just want to give them a fighting chance."

Her deadpan was perfect. I busted out laughing while she continued to sip her Coke, looking like Molly the Mass-Murderer.

My laughter died down, and she slurped again. "Okay, now you're starting to freak me out. Can we talk about something else?"

"Fine." She broke her stare and set her Coke on the bar top. "What do you want to talk about?"

"I have something I want to show you. Wait here." I hurried away from Alex and her psycho persona and headed for the storeroom again. When I came back, I held an item I had hidden in one of the back corners. It was wrapped in one of Dan's dish towels, concealing it from the few prying eyes that still remained in the bar.

I set the item down on the bar in front of Alex and pushed it toward her.

"Do you have any idea of what this does?"

Alex eyed me for a second then pushed her glass aside. "A gift? I feel like it's a little early in our relationship. I really shouldn't."

"It's not a gift. I mean, if you want it, I guess you can have it. I didn't think you wanted—"

Alex held up a hand to halt my stammering.

"Take it easy, smooth operator. I'm just kidding."

Alex pulled back the folds of the towel and examined the box I had retrieved from my shop earlier. She squinted at the mess of circuit boards and wires for a few seconds, then her eyes went wide, and she covered it up again, shooting hurried glances over her shoulder to see if anyone had been watching us.

"Have you lost your mind? Where did you find this?"

I shook my head and helped her cover the box, suddenly infected by her panic. "Zoe had a bunch of them stacked in the old bus at the shop. What is this thing?"

Alex peered over her shoulder then leaned in toward me.

"It's a shield generator. One of the hard-wired varieties. Hellions use those to protect things near and dear to their heart. Something like that Cadillac I took a joyride in. The operative word is Hellion." Her voice was a harsh whisper full of urgent frustration. "Any Woebegone with one of these in their possession gets an automatic trip to a torture mart that makes the Wax Worx seem like Disneyland. You need to get rid of that thing and don't get caught or losing your position in The Judas Agency will be the least of your worries."

I swept the box off the counter and hurried it back into Dan's secret room. It would be safe enough in there for now, at least until I had enough time to get rid of it permanently.

When I walked back out to the main area, Alex still sat on her stool, sipping her Coke, looking a little too casual to really be relaxed. I sauntered across from her like a wind-up doll with a stick up his butt and leaned against the bar trying to look cool as well.

After a few seconds of strained silence, I broke the spell with the obvious question.

"What would Zoe be doing with something like that? With lots of them in fact. What could she be trying to protect that wasn't already protected? The shop is reinforced and has withstood more firestorms than I can count. Do you think she is building her own super-black-market center?"

Alex snorted. "Why would she do that? She practically runs your shop, and it's almost too big to fly under the radar as it is. Can you imagine a Zoe-Mart in neon letters with shopping carts and handicap parking?" She laughed. "I'm pretty sure someone would notice that."

I slumped. "So, what then?"

Alex glared into my eyes. "Not—your—business."

She annunciated each word but then she backed down a

little bit. "Well, actually she's storing them in your shop, so I guess it is your business. But you know what I mean."

"I just—"

Alex put her hand on mine and stopped me from finishing the statement. "Let's talk about something else."

I sighed. "Fine."

I couldn't help but notice that Alex didn't pull her hand back. She kept it there, covering my fingers with her warm touch. I swear she had a superpower that short circuited my brain every time she touched my hand. I struggled for anything to say. After a minute, I blurted out the only thing that came to mind.

"Do you think Jake could be working with Simeon for a cure to stay Topside?"

I had no idea why that thought vomited out of my mouth. I hadn't made that connection—possible connection—until that very moment. Either way, it had the exact romantic effect you might expect.

"Are you trying to piss me off right now?"

Alex pulled her hand away, and all I wanted to do was reach over, pull it back, and start over again.

"I'm just saying, it's weird that we ran into him near Simeon's building. It almost feels like too much of a coincidence."

Yup, Rico Suave has nothing on me.

"I don't care what Simeon's doing." Alex gripped her glass so hard her knuckles turned white. Suddenly, I was a little glad my digits weren't within harm's way after all. "I don't even care what Jake is doing. Simeon could offer him the fountain of youth, and I wouldn't lift a finger to stop them. There's only one thing on my radar right now, and it goes choo-choo, bang. Anything else is background noise."

Now it was my turn to recoil. I stood up straight and crossed my arms over my chest. "Are you sure you only want to hear the bang? Maybe we should set up a couple of lawn chairs up on a hill where we can listen to the people scream. I'd hate for you to miss a moment of your masterpiece."

Alex stood out of her stool and slapped a hand onto the bar. "Set it up. I'll bring my pom-poms and a cheerleader outfit."

Before I could say anything else, she swept her arm across the bar, knocking over her half empty glass of Coke and headed for the door.

"Why don't you handle things here? You're good at the whole Lone Ranger thing. I need to get some sleep. I have a lot of disaster to cause in the morning."

CHAPTER THIRTY-FIVE

Despite all the planning and visits, we almost missed the train when we arrived at the rail transfer station the next morning. I would like to take credit for the debacle, but for once, it wasn't me. Alex and I had failed to take into account one key factor. Trains were long—more than one hundred cars long. As it passed its final inspections and got ready to carry on to its destination, the engine was nowhere near the actual train yard. It was more than a mile down the track, and we were on foot. By the time we got there, the train had already begun to creep forward.

We both jumped onto the head locomotive. Alex paused at the base of the stairs and made sure I made it on but didn't hurry up to the cab.

"I need to know you're with me on this." She gave me a thin-lipped stare that said no amount of humor would ease the moment.

"You're my partner. I'm backing you, no matter what." Alex nodded, and I waited until she turned away to say, "Even if I don't agree with what you're doing."

She didn't hear that last part, of course. The wind and the

sound of the roaring diesel engines drowned out all except the loudest of noises.

Alex got to the access door to the engineer's compartment, counted to three, and then jerked the handle open. I half hoped it would be locked. Assumed it would be. Who drives a gazillion pound train without locking the doors? Even soccer moms lock their doors when they drive to the grocery store.

Alex rushed up the stairs and had the first guy in an arm lock, holding her Luger to his head before I cleared the platform. He wore blue-striped overalls and sported an actual engineer's cap. The second guy, a portly man in rugged blues and round, gold rimmed glasses, stood back from his control panel and put his hands up.

"Down the stairs." Alex sounded so wild and desperate that I followed her instructions before Glasses and Overalls. Glasses came down behind me, and then Alex clambered down with her captive.

We all stood outside the cab, perched on the locomotive's outer walkway. Everyone held onto the railing, trying to compensate for the train's movement and the vibration of the tracks as we gained speed. "Are there any other staff members on the train? Anyone who can stop this thing?" Alex shouted over the roar of the diesel engines.

Glasses looked at his partner, and I saw the panic bloom in their eyes.

"You can't do this." Glasses shouted back. He must have been the actual engineer. "The throttle's set to accelerate. It will keep going until ..." His eyes went up the track as if he could see Bozeman miles over the horizon. "It won't stop."

Alex's grin made me sick to my stomach.

"Keys." She let go of the safety rail and held out her hand, keeping the Luger leveled at Glasses and his partner. When Glasses didn't move to do anything, she clarified. "Give me the keys to the door, now."

Comprehension dawned on Glasses' face, and he fumbled with a keyring at his waist, singling out a key. She took it, jammed the key into the lock, and after securing the door, stood back and stomped the ring with her foot, breaking the key off in the lock to ensure no one could re-enter the cab once we were gone. The finality sent a chill up my spine. Before anyone said another word, Alex reared back again and planted a boot on Overalls' hip and shoved him off the train.

I leapt off behind him, rolling with the impact. We had gained some significant speed, and it was more than a little difficult to find my feet before Overalls got up to run away. Turned out I didn't need to worry. He hobbled several steps on what looked like a sprained ankle, then hopped to a stop. He wouldn't be running sprints anytime soon.

I caught up to him within a few steps and helped him over to where Alex and Glasses now stood. They appeared no worse for wear. Alex still had her Luger, and Glasses seemed a little ruffled but otherwise uninjured.

Alex reached into her back pocket and pulled out a hand full of zip ties. After securing their hands behind their backs, we sat them down next to the tracks and bound their ankles as well. We were already well out of town, so it would be some time before anyone came looking for them. But when they did, they wouldn't be hard to find. It was a nice day, and the cloud cover would keep the sun from beating down on their heads. They would be fine until the cavalry arrived.

Alex and I stood back watching the rail cars go by. I couldn't bring myself to look at her. Even though I knew, or at least hoped, I had done enough to sabotage Strough's Bridge and bring the train down before it ever made it to the town, Alex didn't know that. She still thought this rolling juggernaut was on its way to destroy half of Bozeman.

I crossed my arms and fought to suppress my grin. Enjoy

your moment now because in a couple of hours everything will come crashing down—literally.

The cars accelerated at a deceptive pace. If we had been any later, there was no way we could have run it down and jumped on. The power of something so massive was more than a little impressive, even in the light of the impending tragedy.

I turned to see the end of the line as the last cars came into view. They were not empty coal cars like the rest but rather a group of boxcars, probably full of mining equipment and supplies ordered for the operation.

We stood near the tracks getting a close look at the cars as they passed. When the boxcars finally rolled by, the open doors did not reveal supplies, but instead the faces of hundreds of people.

I tensed and stared in disbelief before staggering toward the train. I jogged at first, then broke into a dead run, arms outstretched to latch on, but the cars were already moving too fast. I was helpless to do anything. Six cars in all, every one filled with people packed like cattle. As I slowed, something else fell into place in my mind. The well-dressed man at the trainyard. The one who hadn't seemed to belong. I now realized why he had seemed so familiar.

My cousins had done the same thing. When I was alive, they worked in the human trafficking business, and I had gotten tangled in it as well. In the end, I snuffed out their trafficking ring along with their lives, but they had guarded their merchandise the same way. Snakes among the workforce, ensuring their product arrived unspoiled.

As the last car pulled away, and I loped to a stop, all the blood drained from my face. These were human slaves, traded for who knew what. All they wanted was a better life, and I had just sentenced every one of them to death.

CHAPTER THIRTY-SIX

I sprinted back to where we had left the engineer and conductor zip tied next to the tracks. Alex still hovered in my way, but I didn't have time to care.

I shoved her aside and jerked Glasses up by his collar, forcing him to stand on his toes. "Tell me how I can stop that train."

He looked down at his partner and then back at me again. His face was flushed with fear, and I saw the confusion in his eyes.

I shook him until words began fumbling out if his mouth.

"I don't know. I-I thought you wanted it to be a runaway. There's no way to stop it."

I threw him back down to the ground and thought about picking up his partner, but it would do no good. Even if we could teleport ourselves onto the platform of the locomotive, Alex had broken the key off in the door. No one would get in there without a crowbar or a sock drawer's worth of C-4.

I clamped my hands to the side of my head and paced back and forth, then faced Alex. I intended to tell her about the people on board and the sabotage that was about to kill them all. I would tell her that I didn't care about her position in The Agency or mine and that we had to find a way to stop that train. I reached out to grab Alex by the shoulders then stopped. Alex had her hands clasped over her mouth, holding back a bout of sobs. Her eyes were a mess of mascara and tears, and she stared at me with an expression so full of sadness and fear that I had to pause.

"What have we done?" Her voice came out high and cracked. "We ... I just sent that train into a town full of people ... and now all those others. Gabe, I don't know what I was thinking."

The tears ran down her face in long lines of anguish, and she bent at the knees as if she could hardly muster the strength to stand.

I hurried over to catch her, holding her up in my arms.

"What are we going to do?" she sobbed. "We have to stop it. I can't believe I was so blinded by my own selfishness. I'm so sorry. And I forced you to follow me." More sobs wracked her chest as she buried her face in my shoulder. "Why didn't you stop me? Why didn't you send me straight to the Gnashing Fields, if that's what it took? I would rather suffer in the pools that cause all this ..."

She broke off unable to finish the sentence.

I tensed, bracing myself for what I was about to tell her. I had no idea how she might take it, but we were rapidly running out of time if we had any chance at all for us to save the people stowed away in the boxcars.

I took her by the shoulders and pushed her away from my chest, forcing her to look me in the eyes.

"I have good news, and I have bad news. I won't bother you with which you want first. You are getting the good. That train will never make it to Bozeman. I came back last night and sabotaged a bridge several miles ahead of the city. The train should derail there and collapse into a very deep gorge before it gets anywhere near a dense population."

Alex stared at me for a minute, letting the meaning of my words sink in, then she grasped both sides of my head and kissed me. It was not a passionate kiss, but the shock of it almost made me fall backward. When she let go, I had to back step to keep my balance. Then she hauled off and slapped me hard enough to rattle my teeth out of my skull.

My hand went to my face as the stinging pain shot from my jaw to my eye and halfway through my brain. Then she grabbed my head and kissed me again. This time when she let go, I put my hands up in defense.

"I've never heard of slap-gratitude, but the second half sucks."

"How could you go behind my back like that?" She raised her hand again, shaking her head. "Thank you so much for doing it, but so help me if you ever do that again."

"Okay, I get it. There is still the bad news part of this equation, remember?"

Realization dawned on Alex's face. She had seen all the people go by as clearly as I had.

"We have to stop that train."

An idea hit me, and I turned back to the two men still sitting next to the tracks. They looked like they had just witnessed an ostrich playing battle chess with a dinosaur. Fear, a whole lot of confusion, and bucketsful of desperation colored their faces. They wanted nothing more than to be rid of us, but before we let them go, I needed information. If I was correct, we might still be able to help the people on the train. I didn't think Alex would like the idea, but our options were limited. We just needed a truck, a little hardware, a high pain tolerance, and we would be in business.

CHAPTER THIRTY-SEVEN

W e had to jog a couple of miles to find a usable vehicle at the rail station. Alex hotwired a maintenance truck, and, as luck would have it, there was a frontage road that ran parallel to the train track, allowing us to catch up and even get ahead of the speeding locomotive.

"Are you sure this is going to work?" Alex did her best to adjust the fall harness strapped around her legs and torso. We had found two of them in the bed of the truck and made quick use of them. Safety third, that's what I always say. Alex had the harness situated over her long coat, making it bunch in all the wrong places, but at least she didn't have to leave it behind. My brown and orange patchwork Gore-Tex fit closer to my body, so the heavy, yellow straps were easier to cinch down and get into place.

"I think we'll have better luck on the cab." I clambered on top of the truck, which we had parked a few feet from the tracks, and helped Alex up behind me. The metal loops on the front of our safety harnesses were now connected to a long length of chain, which threw off our balance, so I hefted the other end, testing the weight.

"No, I'm definitely not sure this is going to work. I am no physicist. We might be dragged under the wheels and torn in half. If you don't want to come, now's the time to jump off the see saw. It's going to get rough either way."

Alex said something, but I couldn't hear as the train went barreling by in a roar of titanic sound and vibration. Wind buffeted our faces, almost knocking us off the top of the truck. Being parked this close to the speeding behemoth was more than a little intimidating, but it was necessary if we were going to try and catch it—literally.

I started to swing the loose end of the chain in a slow arc, trying to time the rhythm of the cars speeding by. I only had one chance at this. If I missed and the chain fell between the cars or got dragged down to the bottom—I shuddered. It was something I didn't want to think about.

Alex put her arms around my waist, bracing for the inevitable impact, and shouted in my ear. "I'm with you. Let's do this."

I threw the chain, and the links sailed through the air, almost in slow motion. I saw the angle of the hook, the slackened S-curve of the chain, then it caught the mounted access ladder on the hopper car, and everything went white.

I was not prepared for the impact of the train yanking us off our feet. Our harnesses spread the shock out across our entire bodies, but I still felt broken bones, lacerations, and dislocated joints ... pretty much everywhere. We dangled on the side of the speeding train, banging helplessly against the steel wall of the hopper car. Neither of us could reach out to steady the relentless pounding. All we could do was wait while our bodies mended themselves. Joints popped back into place, and bones realigned with excruciating efficiency, while internal organs repaired themselves like overworked clay. It all felt like being a Barbie in the hands of a destructive preschooler. All torn apart, just to be shoved back together in all the wrong ways. As soon as I was able to move, the pain got real. I felt every last injury, and it was as if they competed to outdo each other for my attention. My skull, my pelvis, both legs, and my left arm, plus all my ribs. I couldn't breathe, and I felt like everything had disconnected from primary motor control.

Alex hung on the ladder next to me, chained to my side. She had one arm wrapped around the rail staring at me, but not seeing me with blood filled eyes. I couldn't help but look away. I hoped there was no cap on The Judas Agency health coverage plan that allowed us to heal when we were Topside, because we were exercising the limits of its ability right now.

After a few more seconds, Alex let out a groan that grew into a guttural scream, then she wrapped her other arm into the ladder, securing herself to the train as it whizzed across the countryside.

"Better?" I offered a weak smile even I didn't believe.

"That was the dumbest idea I've ever heard of," she shouted over the din of howling metal and wind. "Much less followed through on."

"Hey, I offered to jump from the speeding truck, while you drove, but you wanted to come along."

Alex cracked her neck and started loosening the chain on her harness.

"We would've crashed long before you got on the train, then neither of us would be here."

She pulled the loosened chain through the loop at her chest and handed it to me so I could do the same.

"So, you're saying I had a *good* idea."

I made it more of a statement for entertainment sake. As soon as the chain was loose, I tossed it away and watched the heavy length fall overboard in an explosion of dust and dirt next to the tracks.

"I'm saying shut up and move before this train gets to your bridge and we're out of time."

Alex turned her head into the wind to keep the hair out of her face then started to climb the ladder.

"I think you're saying it was a good idea," I shouted up to her, loud enough to be heard over the noise. "That's okay, you don't have to thank me now. We can talk later."

I started to follow her up, and Alex tapped me on the top of me head with her boot a little harder than was necessary. "Oops. Must have slipped. Be careful not to get boot in your mouth."

I grinned. All healed up and back to normal. That Topside health plan was pretty amazing.

We made our way back to the section where we had seen the people packed into the boxcars. It wasn't far. I had purposely waited for most of the train to pass before I threw the yank-o-blaster that attached us to the passing cars. It was a gamble, but I didn't want to navigate a mile's worth of empty hopper cars to find the back of the train.

We didn't bother to enter the cars themselves, instead we dropped down between them and the last coal hopper and examined the coupler that held them together.

"The engineer said to find the cut bar," I shouted. "Something that pulls the pin holding the coupler. He said it would be under pressure, so it wouldn't be easy to move."

Alex pointed to a greasy pole leading from the coupler to the corner of the car. "Is that it?"

Wind buffeted the two of us from below the cars as we reached down to pull on it. The bar didn't move.

"I'm guessing this is it. Help me jerk this thing up."

Alex hopped around to the boxcar side, and we both got our hands around the bar and braced our feet against the coupler and pulled. We faced each other, so we were able to each give it everything we had.

As first nothing happened, then the pin moved the slightest bit.

"I think we can get it," I shouted. "On three, jerk hard. One, two, three!"

We jerked, and it moved a few more millimeters.

"Again. One, two, three ... One, two, three ...one, two ..."

On three, the pin came loose, and the coupler began to open. It looked like the hands of two star-crossed lovers letting go for the last time. The couplers opened slowly as the locomotive pulled the front half of the train away. The brake line stretched below and then let out a loud hissing bang as it disconnected.

"We did it!" I shouted. Relief poured through me.

"Gabe!" Alex pointed down.

That's when I realized I was standing on the wrong part of the train—the part heading toward its demise.

I leapt for the boxcar side, and Alex's outstretched arms, just as the air brakes engaged, bringing the huge steel undercarriage to a screaming halt.

It took several seconds for us to stop completely. When we did, the silence was almost deafening, like the whole world had stopped to celebrate our victory. The main part of the train made its way down the track toward its fatal destiny, and no one yet knew about our attempted terrorist event. All was peaceful, and we had saved the day.

I jumped down off the car, then helped Alex down as well. Adrenaline surged through me. I couldn't help myself. I turned to wrap her in a big hug and spun her around.

She laughed. "Easy there, Butch Cassidy. Let's get back to those people."

We made our way to the first box car together. I couldn't stop smiling. Even after everything that had happened, we were going to save a literal trainload of human trafficking victims. How could anyone not be happy about that?

I glanced at Alex and saw that she smiled too.

"Shut up," she said when she caught me grinning at her. "I can be happy about doing something good."

I nodded and looked forward again. "I'm just surprised to hear you say it."

I put my hand on the handle of the boxcar door.

"Ready?"

Alex nodded, and I yanked the handle, anxious to see the looks on the people's faces as they poured out of the car. The door slid to the side with a rumble in its tracks and … nothing. Alex lost her smile, and her shoulders fell so far I thought they might slide all the way to her elbows.

I took a step to the side so I could peer into the car and saw a pair of men holding guerrilla style AK-47s. The doors to the other boxcars opened as well, and more men jumped out. I should have known. These desperate people were like gold to the lowlifes who controlled them, and no one shipped gold without guards.

CHAPTER THIRTY-EIGHT

W e both put our hands up, more for the sake of the other people than ourselves. Neither of us wanted some trigger-happy Neanderthal to start shooting and hit an innocent by accident. We would heal. They wouldn't.

"Can we talk about this?" I pointed to the two of us and smiled. "You may not believe this, but we just saved your lives."

I left out the part about us being the ones who put their lives in danger in the first place. Some details were best left unsaid.

One of the guards stepped forward, speed sputtering a language I did not understand. Spanish by the sounds of it, but it may as well have been ancient Hindu for all I knew. He wore a yellow plaid shirt and had a greasy baseball cap with the bill curled so tight it looked like a tube on the front of his forehead. I couldn't help but think of a weird unicorn. The rest of the coyotes all seemed to have one sort of bad hat choice or another as well. One wore a hole riddled beach hat, another a fedora that looked like it had gone through a trash compactor. Still another fancied himself a cowboy, although his hat seemed far too pristine among the hard-ridden attire the others wore.

Unicorn Bill poked his gun in our direction and spouted something again. His posse laughed and that made the little anger hairs stand up on my neck.

"I said, we saved your lousy skin." I raised my voice and annunciated each word as if that would bridge the language barrier somehow. "Why don't you run that way? We'll go this way, and everyone goes wee-wee-wee all the way home?"

Unicorn Bill tilted his head and showed us a grin full of gold and rot. I had never seen such a dental dichotomy in my entire life. Without saying a word, he pulled the trigger and shot me in the shoulder, spinning me around, and landing me on my knees.

I felt my body healing almost instantly, but the bullet still felt like molten iron shot out of a cannon. I waited a moment for the pain to subside, then stood back up behind Alex.

Unicorn Bill and his bad hat brigade stood back in shock. Their human cargo took notice as well. That was not a good thing. Guns or no guns, the bad guys were outnumbered at least twenty to one. If the captors were seen as weak, the people might rebel, and Unicorn Bill couldn't have that. He would fill us full of holes and leave us for dead in the prairie before he allowed that to happen. I knew the type. I had been around them most of my life.

Of course, they didn't know we were all but impossible to kill. Pulling those triggers would start a graphic horror show that would lead to questions ... and a lot of dead coyotes.

"I think now might be a great time for you to exercise your Topside power," I whispered in Alex's ear. "Don't you?"

Unicorn Bill rounded up his hit brigade and raised his arm. Definitely a signal to get ready.

I waved both of my arms. "Wait, wait ... wait. Last request?"

I put my hand to my lips and made a smoking motion with

my fingers then out of the side of my mouth to Alex I said, "I know you don't remember, but I've seen you infuse your power into a gun. It was your gun, but I bet you can heat up their guns too."

Unicorn Bill laughed and shook his head. He reached into his breast pocket and pulled out a pack of cigarettes and threw them at my feet.

"I have no idea how to do that," Alex snapped. "How am I supposed to do something I don't remember?"

I bent over, picked up the pack, and popped a cigarette into my mouth. I laid one hand on Alex's shoulder for support and made a lighter motion with my other hand.

"Just concentrate and imagine all your firepower being channeled into their guns. I'm here for you." I poured every ounce of my own energy into her. It was all I could do. Other than that, it was up to her.

I felt Alex's muscles draw tight under my hand as she drew her brow together in concentration. Her head dipped ever so slightly, and she began to quake as if the strain of her power were almost too much to control.

Unicorn Bill pulled out a lighter, still grinning with that rotten, gold smile. He flicked his Bic, and every firearm in the group burst into flame.

Not just a little flame, like flares off the surface of the sun. Bouts of molten heat consumed the stocks and melted the barrels. Lucky for the guards, the flames had also snapped every gun strap, allowing them to drop their bubbling hunks of slag before they turned into human candles as well.

My cigarette hung off my bottom lip, like a dried twig, as my jaw fell open in shock. The astonished expression on Alex's face told me she was equally as surprised. Unicorn Bill and his Hat Brigade were too busy dancing around to notice as they patted and rolled on the dirt, fighting to put out clothing fires.

When they stopped to look at us again, I snapped my jaw shut and gave them a knowing grin.

Alex still had her arms hanging halfway in the air, unable to recover from her shock as fast as I had. I pulled them down then made the flicking motion with my fingers again and winked. I motioned for them to put their hands up. Language barrier or not, they got the message.

"I think someone's been holding out on me. A little overkill, but I don't think these guys will be picking up a gun anytime soon."

Alex's expression grew from shock to a grin as I motioned for the passengers in the first boxcar to get out. They did, and our new captives got in to replace them. I slammed the door shut and pointed to the latching mechanism.

"Care to do the honors?"

Alex walked over to the car and used her power, this time through direct contact, to melt the mechanism into unusable goo. "The cops will have to cut those guys out when they find them."

I looked over the bewildered looking crowd still standing near the train. "You're free. Those guys won't bother you anymore." I made a shooing motion with my hand. "Get going before someone official shows up and has to do their job."

The rest of the captives got out and began to migrate away from the tracks. They all had little to no belongings. I had seen it many times before. We hadn't given them much of a head start, but at least they weren't under the thumb of a lowlife trafficker. They had a chance to make it, and that was better than no chance at all.

Alex and I watched them go in silence, feeling a mix of triumph and sorrow. I didn't know what would become of them, but I hoped they would do well.

A noise came out of the east, and I turned my head in that direction. A low boom. At first, I thought it was the train hitting the gorge, then I realized it was something much worse. Thunder. I peered up. The clouds I had noticed earlier had banded together, and the show was about to begin. With everything going on today, Alex and I hadn't paid attention to the weather. Now that guns and bad guys were on the bottom of our worry list, meteorological concerns had snuck up to top the charts. I could even smell the rain. We would not outrun this one.

We both darted for the open box car and jumped inside just as the first drops started to fall.

"I sure hope this thing is watertight." Alex peered up at the roof, looking for leaks.

I didn't bother. We were stuck, and there was nothing we could do about it. We just had to pray the storm blew over before anyone thought to look for the missing boxcars at the end of the line. In the meantime, we sat down together to stare at a sight neither of us had seen in years. A deadly rain shower —this time as seen from the negligible safety of an old boxcar.

CHAPTER THIRTY-NINE

We clinked glasses, and Dan filled us up one more time with a fresh spritz of Dr. Pepper. It was a celebration, after all. We rescued the people on the train, captured a bandit ring of human traffickers, and saved Bozeman, Montana from ruin. Of course, we were the ones who had planned to ruin it, but that point seemed moot. Everyone came out of the great, derailing disaster unscathed ... Well, almost everyone. That railway would be out a few dollars. Turned out my little rust job did the trick and then some. The entire train, and all its empty coal cars, wound up in the bottom of that ravine. I had to imagine eco-organizations all over the world were toasting to that little setback. That route would be out of service for quite a while. The power industry would make up for it though. They would double prices, and everyone would keep watching their cable TV and talking on their robot phones. I really needed to talk to Alex about getting one of those Android things. They sounded so cool.

"What did you do with the guys you locked in the rail car?" Dan was so enthralled with the whole story he had forgotten about all his other customers in order to listen to us.

"We left the authorities a very nice note." Alex clinked her glass to mine again. "We explained who the guys were and why they were there. We may have even insinuated that they had something to do with the runaway train."

Dan let out a hoot of laughter. "Serves them right. Bastards like that deserve an express ticket to the pools."

"I'm sure they'll find their way here before they know it. The hard part was cleaning up all the slag Alex left in her wake."

Dan's eyes went wide with wonder. "Yeah, tell me how you burned them again."

Alex laughed. "I have no idea how I did it." She glanced over at me. "I swear you supercharged me somehow. It was like I heard your voice then everything was effortless. Melting the locks was ten times harder, and I had my hands directly on them."

I shrugged. "I guess I'm just your lucky charm. Now you have to keep me around."

Alex smiled at me in a way that made me want to stop breathing. "You are the worst sort of lucky charm. At least as far as The Judas Agency goes." She put her hand on mine, electrifying my skin. "Nothing seems to go wrong around you. Catastrophes cross the street when they see you coming."

Now it was my turn to laugh. "Tell it to my insurance agent. I'm usually the trouble magnet in a Three Stooges film."

Alex shook her head. "You stopped the train, kept that virus from hitting the population a few months ago. We even stayed out of the rain and missed the firestorm raging outside right now. It's like you are a shield and nothing around you can get hurt."

"Speaking of trouble." I turned to Dan again. "Whatever happened with that painting drop? You never told us how it went."

"Gastrith never sent anyone to pick it up. Waited over an

hour for nothing. Someone is supposed to meet me tonight. I'm going to head out as soon as this firestorm blows over."

"Seems like we've had a lot of them lately." Alex took another sip of her drink. "If they get any worse, I am going to have to start carrying a meteor umbrella as a shield."

I laughed. "If someone invents something like that, let me know. I'll take a dozen ..."

I paused, suddenly hit by a realization I hadn't recognized until that moment. Alex saw it in my face as well because she stood up straight and started looking around the bar for trouble.

"What is it? What's wrong?"

I didn't answer. Instead, I rushed into Dan's storage room and came back out with the shield generator I had stashed the night before.

"I thought I told you to get rid of that thing," Alex hissed.

I held out a hand to stop her and turned to Dan. "Did you by any chance turn up any old car batteries when you inherited this place? I know it's a long shot, but I figured since it is made of cars—"

"Yeah. I have a whole bank of them out back. I use them for backup power when the place goes dark."

"Can I borrow one?"

That's all I had to say. He was out and back with a used car battery in less than a minute.

"I think I know what Zoe's up to."

Alex got that *not this again* face, but I shook my head. "This is different. Can we make this thing work?" I held up the generator.

She stared at me for a minute, then it dawned on her what I was asking her to do.

"You mean, you want to go out there right now? In the middle of a firestorm? Have you lost your mind?"

"Can we make it work or not?"

She held her hand up for a second then pulled some of the loose wires over to the battery terminals. It still had the old cable clamps attached, so it gave her something to tie the wires onto. When she was done, I felt a visceral hum that enveloped the area around us.

"I think that's it. Pretty simple really, but I still don't think—"

I grabbed the battery and the generator and headed for the door.

"Hold on a second. If you're going out there, I'm going with you."

Alex reached for her coat, but I kept moving. I hoped I had enough of a head start, but I couldn't be sure. So I sprinted for the door and prayed for the best.

I had to get out and away, so Alex was beyond my shield range. I didn't want her to come with me on this one. It was too much to ask, even of her. If anyone caught me, it would mean more than the end of my career in The Judas Agency. Not just for possession of the generator, but also because of my implied collusion in the crime I suspected Zoe was committing.

Alex cried out behind me. Her voice full of fury and unrestrained malice. I didn't turn around to face her. I couldn't. I set the generator and battery in the rear basket of my tricycle and got on, then I pedaled into the furious storm of fire and brimstone, leaving my partner to rage a whole different storm of her own.

CHAPTER FORTY

F ire rained down around me. Long streams of liquid lava
splashed on roof tops, pooled on the ground, and burned
through just about everything in sight. Brimstone fell from the
sky in all shapes and sizes. Small stone-sized pieces pierced
sheet metal and flesh. Larger Volkswagen-sized chunks crushed
buildings in a single blow. It all sounded like being on the
wrong end of a shooting range full of machine gun maniacs
and grenade launchers. None of it touched me, though. I rode
through it all on my tricycle as it bounced off my impenetrable
shield like burnt cheese off Teflon.

Buildings and Woebegone outside my shield fell alike.
Almost nothing stood up to a firestorm. My shop was one of the
only places that could withstand the onslaught, Dan's bar was
another. Woebegone who got caught out in the open became
toast—literally. The aftermath would result in the wreckage
Scrapyard City was famous for.

This was The Nine, and it did not want its residents getting
comfortable. Firestorms were a great way to keep everyone
lamenting in the Gnashing Fields. When they got out, they
would have just enough time to rebuild before another storm

hit. Smashing hope was always far worse than having none at all, and The Nine was designed to smash hope. Sometimes I forgot how difficult most Woebegone had it here. Seeing this firestorm first-hand drove the point home like nothing else could—almost nothing.

The Wax Worx came into view over the rise—or at least what was left of it. It had stood for as long as I could remember. A symbol of all the horrors and atrocities The Nine had to offer. As I came over the hill, all that remained was a field of burning debris. I could just make out the sign, still half lit with bulbs. It tried to flash its manic pattern, but now it looked more like the shorted-out wreckage of a long-forgotten time.

Flames reached up almost as high as I could see, and I had to squint my eyes against the intense blaze. The impossible tent construction that made up the Wax Worx had gone up like black powder soaked in diesel fuel. If it weren't for my shield, the heat radiating off the incredible pyre would have driven me away. If ever there were a structure that was not meant to standup to a firestorm, it was this one. I had never even thought about the dichotomy. Just another spectacle of power to the Woebegone who suffered all around and especially inside places like this.

Not anymore.

The Skin Quarries had been much less glamorous in architecture—a gigantic warehouse attached to the rear of the tent structure. Even the steel and sheet metal couldn't stand up to the pounding of the storm. It had suffered the same catastrophic fate as the Wax Worx. The entire facility had been leveled to the ground as well. Brimstone and fire pummeled it into a heap of mangled iron. The two facilities represented a burning wreckage miles wide, and I could only imagine how many Woebegone had been inside when it happened. Both places had always been a safe haven from firestorms in the past.

Woebegone would have flocked to their doors when they saw the devastation coming, only to find they were safe no more.

Movement caught my attention to the left. No one should be out in this, including me. But there was a figure watching both establishments burn to the ground. I turned my trike and rode a little closer.

"Zoe?" I yelled, "Is that you?"

The figure turned to look at me then hurried over in my direction. It was definitely Zoe. She wore her dirty, old poncho with the hood pulled up to conceal her face. It was her go-to disguise and seemed to work like a charm. For whatever reason, I almost never noticed her when she was wearing it.

I swung my leg off my trike to stand on the ground, careful not to walk away from the protective confines of my shield. The second she got close, Zoe threw her arms around me and sobbed into my chest.

I held her tight, feeling the relief of seeing her safe in the midst of all that destruction. "Are you okay?"

She wore some sort of backpack under her poncho as well. I felt it when I hugged her close. It was full of a blocky cargo I had to assume was a generator of her own.

She pulled back, tears still running down her cheeks and smiled at me. "I am more than okay. Isn't this wonderful?"

"Wonderful? Zoe, what did you do?"

She looked surprised by my comment. "They're both gone —forever."

"I don't know about forever, but you sure put a dent in their operation. How did you do it?"

I knew the answer but wanted to hear it from her anyway.

Zoe eyed the generator I had wired up in the back of my tricycle. "Looks like you have been rummaging around in my stuff. I was surprised at how many generators were installed in that place. It wasn't easy to get them all out."

"*My* shop, remember? And I don't recall ever signing on to being part of a major terrorist organization."

Zoe snorted. "Have you read the mission statement for The Judas Agency lately?"

"Touché. But that's different."

"Different how? Because someone told you it is? Because you take your marching orders from some demon who says it's okay? I don't think so."

I stopped and took a deep breath. Then after a second, I asked, "What about all the Freshborns trapped in the cages?"

Zoe's eyes went down to the ground. She was silent for a long moment, then said with conviction, "No one will use them as Disposables again."

I shook my head. "And at what cost? They're all suffering in the Sulfur Pools right now. By their perception, they will be there for an eternity. You're no better than—"

Zoe looked up at me. I expected to see anger or maybe even shame in her eyes, but I found neither. She had an almost pitying expression as she tilted her head to speak.

"You know I love you. I appreciate everything you have done for me. I couldn't have survived without you, but I can't stay anymore."

"What do you mean you can't—"

Zoe held up a hand to stop me.

"I can't subscribe to the morals you hold any longer. I can't stand by while you lecture me on maintaining the status quo. I'm not saying those choices can't be right for you. I'm only saying they aren't right for me."

She stepped in on her tiptoes and kissed me on the cheek.

"Don't worry about your shop. Meg and Jazzy are very good at running the place. I haven't mentioned it to you, but they have pretty much taken over while I worked on ... other things."

"Zoe, this is crazy. You can't just—"

She put a finger to my lips and then reached around to give

me a hug. "Don't make this an argument. I want us to part as friends. Thanks for coming. It means a lot to me. I'm glad I got to share this moment with you."

She stood back, paused a minute, then turned to leave, marching out into the firestorm like a bubble in water.

"Wait. Where are you going? When will you be back?"

Zoe turned around but kept walking backward, continuing to withdraw. "I can't tell you where I'm going. It's for your own good. As for when I'll be back ..." She shrugged. "Maybe sometime, maybe never. Doesn't change how I feel about you. Thanks again for everything. Don't worry about me. I'll be all right. And if I'm not, know that whatever happens is my choice."

She smiled, blew me a kiss, and turned to walk away, disappearing into the storm like a bird into the clouds.

CHAPTER FORTY-ONE

The firestorm had subsided by the time I pedaled my way back to Hula Harry's. Shock and guilt coursed through me. I took the long way back, using every moment to think about what I could have done differently, how I could have kept Zoe from going, or how I could have stopped her from repeating her apartment building massacre all over again. I should have done more. If I had been staying at the shop instead of at The Agency, I would have been there for her and could have prevented this from happening. She needed a friend, and I failed.

I still couldn't fully comprehend or even understand what she had done. Yes, many of the Woebegone in the Wax Worx deserved what they got, but the Disposables in the Skin Quarries hadn't. I knew they would come back in time, but Zoe had willfully sent them to unspeakable torture. The Sulfur Pools were a fate worse than death. That's what made the Disposable handlers such horrible monsters. It wasn't just the terrible things they made the Disposables do—all the murder, rape, torture—but the handler's willingness to recycle their Disposables through the Gnashing Fields over and over again that made them truly heartless.

Even though a Woebegone would only vanish for a couple of weeks by our perception, to them it would be lifetimes of unending anguish and misery. The torment was so complete that when a Woebegone emerged, they didn't even know their name. They had no identity or recollection of who they were. The agony tore away all memory, at least for a while, leaving a Freshborn vulnerable to be taken advantage of again. Thus, the cycle of the Disposable was born.

Zoe did have one thing right. The Disposables in that warehouse would be free of the cycle. At least as far as The Skin Quarries were concerned. They would not be back to collect them from the Sulfur Pools. That did not mean some enterprising lowlife wouldn't take their place. This was The Nine. Fill in one cesspool, and you're just digging the hole for another one to form. It never stopped.

I pulled up to Hula Harry's, the only ray of sunshine in this crotch rot of a universe. Dan had a great thing going. A little slice of Heaven among a heaping plate full of Hell.

I swung my leg over my tricycle and reached down to retrieve the shield generator. The firestorm was over, but it would not be good to leave it lying around for someone to steal, or worse, report. The last thing I needed right now was more trouble. All I wanted to do was go inside and make peace with Alex for leaving her behind. Once she settled down, or twisted my nose off, I could tell her what had happened and drown my sorrows in a triple shot of root beer.

As soon as I opened the door to the bar, I knew that plan was out the window. I hurried over and set the generator down on the bar, then joined Alex and Dan at one of his tables. They were the only two people in the place, and it was clear why.

Dan looked like he had been worked over by an industrial

meat grinder and stamped back into a Dan shaped patty. He was broken, bleeding, and bruised in almost any way you could imagine. I wasn't even sure how he could still be breathing.

"What happened?"

Alex shot me glare that would slice Kevlar in two.

"What do you care? Did you have a nice ride through the storm?"

I stared back at her, without even flinching. I had left to protect her. If she wanted to be pissed about that, let her. At this point, I couldn't care less if she was mad.

"Zoe's gone. She destroyed the Wax Worx and the Skin Quarries, along with killing every handler, patron, and Disposable inside. Then she took off. I doubt we'll ever see her again." Saying it all out loud made it feel like a punch in the gut.

Alex stared at me, mouth half open in shock.

"How did she—"

I pointed to the shield generator I'd left on the bar. "She took out all their protection. The firestorm did the rest. When I found her, she was watching the show."

Alex lost her sharp glare, and her eyes went to the ground. "I can't believe it. Especially after we found out about—"

"I know," I said, cutting her off. "Part of me thinks we should have expected something like this, not assume she had changed."

We all sat there for a moment. Alex and I in silence, Dan wheezing in agony.

"So, are you going to tell me what happened here?"

Alex glanced over at Dan. He didn't react more than to look away from her when she made eye contact.

"Just so you know, we're not done talking about how you left me." Alex shot me a hard look then softened her eyes and turned back to Dan. "He went out to make the drop as arranged but his—associate—had a change of heart."

"Bastards snuck up on me from behind." Dan's voice sounded thick and garbled as if his mouth were full of cotton. "Bunch of clowns."

I shook my head. "What kind of lowlifes hit one guy from behind? Did you see what any of them looked like?"

Dan raised an eyebrow on his swollen face. "Yeah. I just told you. They were a bunch of clowns."

I blinked. "Wait, you mean they were literally a band of face-painted circus freaks?"

Dan bobbed his head and then winced at the action. "That's what I'm telling you. They worked me over, took the painting, then said Gastrith would be back at midnight to tear the place down. I guess his protection plan had an expiration date."

I let that sink in for a few seconds while Alex did her best to keep Dan comfortable. I closed my eyes, took a few breaths, then stood, grabbing a nearby glass and threw it across the room.

It hit one of the shelves behind the bar and shattered not only itself, but also a half empty bottle of Bacardi Rum. I wanted more things to throw, more things to break, but in a bar made of steel, there weren't many options. I stood up and hurled my chair in the opposite direction, taking a few tables and chairs with it, then I drove my fist into the tabletop in front of me several times, ignoring the pain that shot up my wrist and all the way into my arm.

I waited for Alex to chastise me for my tirade, but she just sat there next to Dan, rubbing his hand.

"Thanks," Dan said, after a few minutes of watching me huff over the table. "I wanted to do that, but my thumbs don't work."

I coughed out a laugh, then Dan and Alex let out a bout of tense laughter as well.

"So, now what do we do?" I said, still too frustrated to find a chair and sit down again.

"There's nothing we can do." Alex offered a sympathetic smile as if she were giving a family terminal news about a loved one. "We can't fight a demon, especially a high-level demon. They're too powerful. We would be like ants on a log to him. All we can do is get out of the way and hope he doesn't decide to come after us. After that stunt we pulled at the warehouse, we'll be lucky if all he does is tear the bar down."

"You mean ..."

Dan nodded. "It was all Gastrith's idea in the first place. That was his warehouse. He already had the painting. He just wanted us to give it back."

My hands went to my mouth, and I started to sit down, even though there was no longer a chair to sit on behind me.

Alex rushed around and slid one under my butt as my balance teetered, and I crashed onto the seat thinking about all the damage I had caused to that warehouse. Because of me, Bug Face had utterly destroyed the place and everything in it. If Gastrith got his hands on me, he would drag me through a razorblade forest and dip me in lemon wedges. Alex was right. If he just tore down the bar, we should count ourselves lucky. But I was never one to depend on luck.

"We should get out of here." I did my best to sound concerned and understanding, but underneath, my nerves were on fire with urgency. I looked at Dan. "You can stay at my shop tonight ... for as long as you like. We'll settle you in there, then you and I should head back to the Agency before tall, clown, and ugly comes looking for us. The more distance we can put between us and Dan, the better. Maybe Gastrith will think we were acting on our own."

Alex pulled her lips into a thin line and shook her head. "Not likely. Why would he think we were trying to steal the painting on our own?"

I shrugged. "I know it's thin, but it is all we have. At least Dan should be safe in my shop tonight. I doubt anyone will find him there."

Alex agreed and stood up. "Come on, bruiser. Let's get you moving. You can sit on Gabe's wonder trike, and we'll push you."

Dan stood up with a little help from Alex and shook his head. "I am not getting on that thing. I may be hurt, but I still have my dignity."

Alex snorted out a laugh.

"Fine," I said. "That's the thanks I get for putting you up in my place."

Dan put an arm over Alex's shoulder, and I hurried over so he could put his other one over mine. "If I have a choice between riding that silly-cycle and staying here, I would rather take my chances here."

Alex laughed again. "I'm glad to see they couldn't bruise your sense of humor."

We were just about to walk out the door when I paused. "Hold on a second."

I made sure Dan was situated on Alex for balance, then I hurried back to the storeroom. When I came out, I had the shield generator along with the small transport device Alex and I had installed that allowed Dan to receive his stock of precious soda from the School for the Blind.

"Can't have these falling into the wrong hands." The finality of removing the transport device hit home in a way walking out the door had not. Those clowns may not have bruised his sense of humor, but I had just hit him where it hurt. His sense of reality. Taking that transporter meant it was over. This place, his endeavor to add a ray of hope to this nightmare, was finished.

I wanted to tell him it wasn't. I wanted to tell him not to lose hope, but I couldn't. The idea I had playing out in my brain was too crazy—even for me to believe in. Besides, if I told Dan I planned to come back and do battle with that demon, Alex would want to come with me, and I couldn't allow that. Suicide was one thing. Hauling your partner along for the ride was another. She would be furious when I left her a second time, but there was nothing to be done about it. I just hoped my ace in the hole would come out to help me play.

CHAPTER FORTY-TWO

I had no idea if demons ever slept. I didn't know if they had to eat, rest, workout, or tell jokes to keep their demon spirits from getting down in the dumps. I just knew every time I visited Judas's office, Procel stood in that same spot in the corner like an immovable pillar of granite. I had spoken to him on a few occasions. Mostly when he came to collect me for Judas, which involved many ... many threats of bodily harm. This time, however, I hoped Procel had a softer side, or at least one I could bargain with.

After we dropped Dan off at my shop, Alex and I headed back to the Agency to turn in for the night. I, however, headed straight for the top floor of Judas's building. Much to my surprise, Judas's secretary still sat at her desk, diligently mark-ing, stamping, and sorting paperwork of some kind. Anything to ensure she did not have to turn her attention to me.

If she was here, it could mean Judas was here as well. If that were the case, I might as well walk out the top story window right now. He would not appreciate any part of my plan to save Hula Harry's, and he'd like my idea to involve his bodyguard even less. Oh well. I walked all the way to Piranha Lake to go skinny dipping; I could at least test the water.

As I approached, his secretary eyed me without saying a word, still shuffling and sorting papers on her desk without looking at them.

"What can I do for you Mr. Gantry?"

"Hi ... hello. I'm just wondering if the big guy is in. I know it's a little late but—"

"It is very late. No one in their right mind would be in the office at this hour, including Mr. Iscariot."

I paused, not sure whether that meant he was out or that he was in and she was disgruntled about it. She must have picked up on my confusion because she sighed and looked down at her desk again.

"No, he is not in. I'm sure he'll be here bright and early in the morning, as will I, but I think we both know you aren't interested in talking to Mr. Iscariot."

I stared at her trying to work my mouth into some sort of response.

"Don't bother with an excuse. As I believe I have mentioned before, I am Judas Iscariot's personal assistant. I know why you're here. It's my job to know pretty much everything; although, I find it prudent to withhold some details from Mr. Iscariot ... for his own good. He likes to break things, and I don't like to clean up his office after he hears about half-witted attempts to save a useless establishment from destruction."

She held up a crumpled piece of paper and waved it in the air. All I saw were the words memo and Hula Harry's.

"How did you ..."

"The answer would literally make your brain explode. Your opportunity to enlist some assistance is about to leave. You can either waste time talking to me or get in there and do what you came here to do."

She stopped sorting papers and peered at me over her horn-rimmed glasses.

"Someday," I pointed at her, "you and I are going to have a long and meaningful conversation."

She went back to her paperwork as I backed away from her desk and headed for Judas's office door. "Not so far as I can tell, Mr. Gantry."

I wanted to say something else, but I had a feeling I would lose my opportunity to talk to Procel if I did, so I turned around and raised my hand to knock on the door instead.

As usual, the door opened on its own, and I walked in, peeking around the corner, not quite convinced that his secretary had told me the truth.

Sure enough, Judas's empty desk was flanked by a very tall demon on one side and another, smaller, much more scary predatory demon opposite him. Judas himself was absent.

I didn't want to plead my case in front of Mastema, but there was nothing to be done about it. I doubted Procel would be up for a chat at the local coffee shop. I walked in, eyeing her as she tracked me crossing the room. It unnerved me the way she did that with a blindfold on. She knew it too by the way she grinned while she did it.

When I got to Judas's desk, I edged in Procel's direction and lowered my voice hoping only he would be able to hear me.

"Hey there, big guy. I hope I haven't caught you sleeping or anything." I smiled trying to break some of the tension. Procel did not look down, grin, or even flinch in my direction. He just stood there like a winged mountain of detachment.

"Yeah ... well, I came here to ask a favor. It's a pretty big one, so feel free to say no—"

"No."

Procel's voice boomed throughout the office like a cannon going off. I ducked like I was being assaulted with machinegun fire.

"Wait, hold on. You haven't even heard what the favor is yet."

"It does not matter. You told me I was free to say no."

I pinched the bridge of my nose while Procel stood there mountainous as ever.

"All right. Wait until I ask the favor first, then please give me an honest answer."

I looked up at him. His face was deadpan as ever, but he didn't say anything. So I took that as an invitation to continue.

"I have a friend, a very good friend, who is about to be assaulted unjustly by a high-level Hellion. I'm willing to fight for him, but I think we both know how that's going to turn out. This guy is trying to do good down here, and that's what we're about, right? Trying to do the right thing? Why can't we do it in The Nine once in a while too?"

No reaction. Not even a blink. Did he ever blink?

"If you help me, I'll promise you anything you want. You can ask anything of me, and I won't refuse. I will owe you any favor to be repaid at any time. I would offer the same to anyone who would help, it means that much to me, but I am here offering it to you. What do you say?"

Procel stared out over my head as if I weren't there, the way he always did, so I jumped up and down a little and waved to try and get his attention. "Hello, did you hear me? Do we have a deal?"

Procel glanced down at me and took a breath. I held mine, waiting for his answer.

"No."

The air came out of my lungs like a burst balloon. "No? What do you mean no? I just promised everything but my soul to you, and you say no?"

"That is correct. The answer is no."

I stood in front of him, mouth agape, not knowing what else to say.

"Could you give me a reason why?"

"It is not my place to meddle in the affairs of other Hellions."

"What do you mean?" I all but shouted in exasperation. "That is pretty much your job description. You slink around in the dark and collect information so schleps like me can stop bad things from happening." I looked him up and down. "Although, how you manage to sneak anywhere is beyond me."

"Operating in the shadows is my purview under the direction of Mr. Iscariot. Allowing myself to engage in open battle would ... raise questions."

"So that's it then." I threw my arms out in frustration. "You won't do anything unless Judas tells you to?"

Procel went back to his stony persona, staring out over my head again.

"Well, that's just fine. I'm no puppet. I will fight for what's right. I know I'm going to get torn apart, but I'm still going out there to stand between that clown-faced jerk and Dan's bar. At least I'll try instead of standing in a corner waiting for someone to tell me when I can eat, sleep, and pee."

I squinted back at him.

"Do you even pee? Never mind, it doesn't matter. I'm going out there alone, if I have to." I backed out toward the door, keeping my eye on the stony demon. "At midnight ... Hula Harry's ... in case you change your mind."

I paused for a second, hoping for some sort of reaction. None came. I turned my attention to Mastema and nodded in Procel's direction. "I don't know how you live with this guy day in and day out. A barrel of nonstop laughs."

I raised my arm to wave at Procel. "Thanks for nothing, big guy. Glad I wasted my time. Have fun standing in the corner, or whatever it is you do when people aren't around."

I rounded the door then popped my head back into the office unable to resist seeing if Procel had moved. He hadn't.

I sighed and walked out the door.

"Goodbye, Mr. Gantry."

Without even making eye contact, I headed past the reception desk and gave a defeated wave. "Goodbye, Mrs. Whoever."

Frustration and anger washed through me as I stomped onto the elevator. Nothing seemed to be going my way. Zoe was gone, probably for good. Alex was still pissed at me, and now I had to go up against Gastrith and his creepy clown posse all on my own. I couldn't even ask Alex for help. I didn't want to get her killed. Procel had been my last chance. Without him, there was only one thing left to do. Head down to my locker and gear up for a fight I most certainly could not win.

CHAPTER FORTY-THREE

It was almost midnight, and I stood in front of Hula Harry's like a starved coyote driven away from its pack. The Nine had no moon or stars, but nighttime carried with it a strange, reddish glow in the sky. Not like sunset, more like an angry fire deprived of oxygen. Deep and full of hunger. It changed things, made the inhabitants more primal, more evil, and the closer it got to midnight, the more intense the glow became. I made it a rule never to be out in the Blood Glow, but tonight was different. Tonight, I would use it to fuel my hostility.

I was determined to win this fight. Nothing would dissuade me. I would come out on top or die trying. There was no in between—not unless Gastrith took me captive and held me as some sort of torture entertainment. That would be worse ... way worse.

I ruminated on that thought for a moment as I stared out at the long street in front of me. Thoughts of me in a cage, guarded by mimes, made me begin to falter. Who wouldn't falter? Mimes!

I shook off the horror show playing out in my head and

straightened my spine. Mime or no mime, Hula Harry's was a clown-free zone. I tightened my grip on my Whip Crack and made sure it played out free to my right. I had my Knuckle Stunner laced into my left hand. I thought about bringing more creative weaponry from the Agency, but this was what I knew. I was a surgeon with the Whip Crack at midrange, and a baboon could use a Knuckle Stunner up close. I was as ready as I was going to get. Now if the stupid clown posse would just show up before I burned up all my adrenaline ...

"Come on!" I shouted out at no one in particular.

A hand fell on my shoulder, and I spun, swinging the Knuckle Stunner around in a wild arc to hit whoever had snuck in at my back.

"Whoa," came a familiar voice. "Check your chi. The fight isn't even here yet."

Alex stood about six feet away from me. She knew I would swing on her and got out of the path before I so much as twitched. She wore her long coat with the flared sleeves and a knowing grin that only meant one thing. She was armed and ready for a fight. I didn't want to be glad she was here, but every cell in my body cheered for joy.

"What are you doing? You are supposed to be back at the Agency."

"You're supposed to be back at the Agency," she chided in a whiny voice. "I could say the same for you. I thought we were partners. First you take off to go look for Zoe, which I still haven't forgiven you for, then you sneak back here to hog a whole demon fight for yourself. You're a real jerk, you know that? Learn to share."

"How did you know I'd be here?"

"Oh, please." She rolled her eyes.

I wanted to laugh. A chuckle even escaped my lips, but panic overrode the levity.

"They're going to be here any second. You need to get out of here—"

Alex flipped one of the Song Reapers out of her sleeves and had the tip of the blade resting inside of my left nostril before I could blink.

"With Zoe gone, you may have an urge to transfer that big brother *I have to look out for you* vibe onto someone else. I can assure you I am not that person. If you think I'm going to slink home just because you're afraid I might get hurt, you have another thing coming ... like a sinus transplant."

I held my hand up in surrender and did my best not to sneeze. "Message received. Let's save the face amputations for the bad guys."

Alex removed her Kama from my over-stretched nostril and held it down to her side while her second Song Reaper fell into her other hand.

"Actually, I think your friends are here."

I turned my attention up the street and watched what might have been the most disturbing military charge in history. At least three dozen clowns, all of different shapes, sizes, and disciplines, ambled down the road in front of us. Some wobbled, some skipped, some even did cartwheels. It occurred to me that in different makeup, this could have been a band of goblins, or evil penguins, and they would have approached the same way. Well, maybe not the cartwheels.

The good news was every one of them looked to be a Woebegone. That meant the preshow was a fight we could win. Behind them, however, came the main attraction—a twelve-foot demon all decked out in clown regalia. He wore a purple suede jumpsuit with a huge, red ruffled collar. His white head was topped with bright orange horns, and he had a big, red clown nose and a disturbingly large mouth painted from ear to ear. Despite all this, Gastrith's most unsettling feature was his eyes, or rather the absence of them anywhere on his face. It made him look more like a demonic alien than a clown.

He held a staff that was at least as tall as he was. It was difficult to see from this distance, but the top seemed to be the carved head of a court jester, and the little socks of his hat moved and jingled every time Gastrith swung it forward.

All in all, I was quite sure nothing Alex and I had in our arsenal would make a dent in this Hellion's hide. He could flick us out of the way and get on with his demolition with little more than a thought.

He could try.

If this clown liked shows, it was a show he would get.

I marched forward, spinning my Whip Crack into a frenzy of hissing metal blades and then flicked it out at the closest clown who came into range. A mime of course. Darn things were always so quick.

I took off his arm, leaving him alive on purpose, so he would turn tail and run back to his master. The mime let out a very un-mime like scream and took off running, holding his arm at the stump. Gastrith took one look at this and shoved the butt end of his staff through the chest of the retreating clown. He may not have had any peepers, but he wasn't sightless.

The remainder of his gaggle stopped short, lining up in an offensive formation of sorts. Alex and I stood side by side, about six feet apart, giving one another plenty of room to maneuver. The least we could do was take out his entourage. Without an audience, maybe Gastrith would get bored and come back another day. Or maybe he would get super pissed and take out half the town. Either way, I could tell Alex was thinking the same way. All her attention was on the circus freaks ahead of us. When this thing broke loose, we were going to redefine carnage and do it in record time.

"Who dares to stand in defiance of the mighty Gastrith?"

Now this was a character I recognized. A fat, face-painted

clown sauntered up from the line and stepped toward me. He wore a red and white striped jumpsuit covered in pom-poms and had a bright red smile painted over half his face. In his right hand, he bore a bundle of balloons big enough to threaten lift off. This was Pogo the Clown. John Wayne Gacy. The serial killer who lured kids with his little act when he had been alive so he could butcher them in his home. Gastrith's prize possession ... and my prime target.

"Tell your boss he's been paid in full. This place is no longer in need of his protection. Shove off, or my partner and I will turn those grins into a fist haven of missing teeth."

Pogo and the others looked at each other, and I leaned in Alex's direction.

"You know, because they have smiles painted on their faces." I hissed out of the side of my mouth. "I've been waiting to use that one."

"Shut ... up ..." Alex drew the response out into two sharp words, and I straightened again.

"Sheesh, surrounded by a bunch of clowns, and no one has a sense of humor."

"Stand aside," Pogo said, "and you may survive."

"You know, I expected a serial killer to be a little less formal. Maybe even a little simple. What's with all this *stand aside* and *who dares to?* I think maybe you're trying too hard. Just relax and let things happen. I promise to keep you right in the middle of all the action."

I meant for that threat to unnerve him, but a wry grin grew on his face. He looked at me with predatory eyes that had me on my heels instead.

Without saying another word, Pogo held up a finger and then pulled out one of his balloons, offering it to me. When I didn't take it, he shrugged and let go of it anyway. The balloon floated up, and I noticed all the clowns followed its path with a little too much eagerness. You could have heard a pin drop as it floated over our heads then dropped back down outside one of the far automotive bricked walls of the bar. The single balloon stopped there for a moment, as if driven by remote control, then it exploded with a boom that shook the ground beneath our feet. The crushed cars flipped, leaving a gaping hole in the wall. I turned back to see that Pogo was smiling, offering me yet another balloon.

CHAPTER FORTY-FOUR

I moved first, sidestepping Pogo and his bouquet of exploding party favors, putting some distance between us. I saw Alex do the same. I wanted more than anything to cut Gacy down right there, but he was too close. If he decided to detonate his balloons in our face, this hoedown would be over before it started.

I had planned to roll out away from him and then cut away a few of his more necessary appendages with my Whip Crack, but I found the mini Clown army more formidable than I expected.

These jokers were not the usual Woebegone thugs Alex and I ran into. At first, their movements seemed erratic and unorganized, but it only took a few seconds to see there was a method to their madness. Jugglers snaked inside while acrobats worked to flank our position in rapid tumbles and flips. The visual representation looked like total chaos, but within a few breaths, the circus freaks had Alex and I isolated and way too busy to interrupt Pogo's demolition balloon act.

I started to flip my Whip Crack out at one of the acrobats who had managed to sneak in behind me, but I stopped as he tore one of the Pom-Poms off his jumpsuit and hurled it in my direction. I slipped to the left, letting it whiz past my thigh. Behind all that fluffy fringe was a miniature spiked ball. It stuck into the ground, and noxious gas erupted from the tines as well.

As if poison Pom-Poms weren't enough, a pair of jugglers who shared what looked like a hundred balls between them, began hurling them at me with the ambidextrous ease of two-armed big-league pitchers. I managed to sprint a tight arc around them, leaving a trail of explosions in my wake. The second they ran out of ammo, I returned the favor, snapping my Whip Crack out to remove their launch mechanisms altogether. Let's see them try out for Lucifer's Little League with no arms.

The jugglers headed off in a torrent of screams, but I was still outnumbered almost fifteen to one. I stole a quick glance at Alex to see that she was doing considerably better than me. Scores of the painted juggernauts littered the ground around her as she worked her Song Reapers like an acrobatic scorpion. The clowns didn't stand a chance. Next to her, they looked like the bumbling, pie-faced sideshows they really were.

I turned my attention back to my own Big Top Troop and swept my Whip Crack out to disrupt their attempt to regroup. I took out another set of jugglers and four of the flipping Pom-Pom throwers. Their noxious fumes rose into the air in a sick, greenish-yellow haze all around me, and I did my best to avoid it. I'd never run into poison gas in The Nine, but you could bet if they had it, breathing in a lungful would be like swallowing a razor blade value-pack. I closed my eyes and held my breath as I dove through another sickly cloud and took down two more jugglers before they could launch their barrage of colorful hand grenades at my head.

I had just finished off that last set of face painted freaks when another set showed up behind them. These guys had to have one of those crazy cars spitting out clowns somewhere.

This next trio ambled up on oversized shoes, waddling like hobo penguins. When they got within range, they all nodded their over-grinning faces and leaned their lapel flower in my direction.

No way.

I dove to the side only to see bouts of a sticky, yellow liquid hit the ground in a bubbling, steaming hiss. The acid cut deep lines in the dirt and left the air smelling of metallic rot. They coordinated their shots, trying to hem me in, but I rolled again, putting me just out of range. They shuffled forward over the bubbling ground and set themselves up to fire again, but I surprised them by launching myself forward rather than trying to retreat. When they shot their acid flowers again, it went over my head and I swept my Whip Crack in a wide arc, taking out their legs. Their acid supply must have been somewhere between their thighs because the second my blades cut them down, the streams went limp, and the trio fell into a pool of their own melting makeup.

"Gabe, the balloons!"

Alex's voice pulled my attention away from the gooey mess, and I looked toward Hula Harry's. A slow, methodical line of Pogo's floating party demolitions headed straight for the establishment's walls. He continued to lay them out one at a time into the air, beaming with his serial killer's grin. I reached down and picked up one of the spiked Pom-Poms at my feet and hurled it at the lead balloon. It exploded on impact, taking out the one behind it as well.

Pogo laughed and clapped as if this were the most exciting thing he had seen all day, then released another balloon from his fingers.

I had to do something to stop him, but what?

My remaining clown posse had regrouped and were closing in. There were only a few left but enough to keep me busy. Then I got an idea. I sidestepped, putting myself between Pogo and the advancing clown front. I used my Whip Crack to cut down a wayward acrobat seeking to hit me from the side with one of his spikey poison surprises, but I left the final acid spraying trio in front of me for last. As soon as they launched their face eating spray, I sidestepped to watch the show.

Unfortunately for me, the show had been canceled. I had hoped the spray would hit Pogo and his balloons, destroying them all together, but while my back was turned, something else had gotten in the way. Something horrible and unthinkable—a mime. And somehow, he had stopped the acid from reaching Pogo.

The acid trio recognized my ploy, and instead of endangering Pogo again, they drew meat cleavers, cleverly disguised as rubber chickens, and charged. This was the sort of attack I was used to, so I made quick work of them with the Whip Crack, leaving them in rolling chunks long before they got to within a few steps.

With all my attackers disposed of, I turned my attention back to Pogo and his bodyguard mime. I didn't understand how he had warded off the acid attack earlier, but I doubted he would do as well with my hungry blades.

The mime looked at me, keeping up his act. He had his lips pursed into a tight O of surprise as he played the whole *I'm stuck in a box and can't get out* routine.

"Here, let me help you crack that thing open," I shouted, then snapped my Whip Crack straight at his head.

I was disappointed a second time by a lack of impact. Instead of striking the beret-wearing irritation, my Whip Crack hit something solid about twelve inches in front of him and bounced off.

You've got to be kidding. A mime with a real forcefield?

The ground shook with another explosion, and I saw Alex hurling more of the spiked balls at the balloons. Pogo had laid out more than two dozen of them in the air. She had disposed of her clown assault force, and so far, we had kept Pogo's floating demolition parade from reaching the bar, but sooner or later, we were going to run out of those spiky balls and then ... boom. No more Hula Harry's.

I pounded on the Mime's shield again and again with my Whip Crack, but nothing happened.

"See if you can hit Pogo from the other side," I shouted.

Alex launched one of her Song Reapers almost before I finished speaking. It sailed to within about a foot of Pogo's pudgy head then bounced off and landed harmlessly on the ground. The mime responded with mock surprise and completed a lap around Pogo's back completing his invisible box routine in irritating silence.

"Now what?"

Alex picked up another of the spiked balls lodged near her foot and threw it at the furthest balloon, destroying it before it could get to the bar.

I searched the ground for one I could throw. At least we would buy a little time while we came up with an idea. I found one a few feet away and snatched it up. I drew my arm back to launch it forward, then paused, considering for a moment.

"What are you doing? Throw it!"

Alex's voice was a high shriek of panic as she searched for more of the spiked ammunition, but I waited, staring down-range, waiting for the perfect moment. I watched Pogo out of the corner of my eye, then, just when he released a new floating projectile, I turned and launched my spike at him, or rather, his balloon.

The mime stretched his arm out but didn't have the range to protect it. The moment my spikes made impact, they caused a chain reaction. The balloons trailing toward the bar exploded in succession. More importantly, so did the remaining bouquet in Pogo's hands. The confinement of the mime's box contained the detonation just long enough for us to see the gruesome splatter of clown parts on the imaginary walls before they dissolved, and it all fell to the ground in a box shaped shluck of goo. The sight was so gruesome, I had to turn away and hold a hand over my mouth to keep from retching.

"Nooooooo."

A graveled voice came from behind the battlefield. Until now, Gastrith had been content to watch from the sidelines, content to let the Woebegone fight it out for his entertainment, but Pogo's gruesome outburst had hit a chord. He stood up and pointed his staff at me, lowering the jester's head in my direction.

"How dare you defy my will?"

For the first time, I noticed the face on the staff was animated. It looked scared ... no, horrified, as if it were a real person trapped on the head on this Hellion's staff.

He swung it from side to side, and I realized that was how Gastrith saw. The staff—or rather the jester's head on top of it —acted as his eyes.

"You have taken my prize, and now I will take yours."

His staff swept over to where Alex stood.

"Oh, I don't think so, Big Ugly."

I charged him and launched my Whip Crack at the forearm that held the staff. Whirring blades wrapped around his forearm to grind and rasp at the skin but did not chew through. Not all the way at least. Gastrith reached over and untangled the weapon from his arm, throwing it away like a wayward string. I saw where the blades had bitten into him. He was bleeding ... could bleed, but it was little more than a flesh wound.

Gastrith reached out for Alex, but she would not go down without a fight. "You will make a fine addition to my collection ... once you are broken."

She launched her Song Wraiths, but they just bounced off the Hellion's thick hide. She might as well have thrown toothpicks for all the good they had done. His hand wrapped around Alex's neck, and Gastrith hefted her ten feet in the air as if she weighed nothing. She struggled, beating at his wrists, but to no avail.

"Yes, a nice addition indeed."

Gastrith turned his attention to Hula Harry's as if I weren't even there. "But first, this."

He took a couple of steps toward the bar, passing me without a thought. I decided to remind him. I wrapped my Whip Crack around his neck from behind and pulled as hard as I could. The demon gagged, stumbling backward. He threw Alex against the outside wall of the bar out of surprise, and her head crashed into the heavy, crushed cars. She didn't move after that. She laid limp and still on the ground.

"You bastard! If she's hurt I'm going to tear you—"

I never got to finish my threat. Gastrith simply reached back, plucked me up by my throat, then unwrapped my Whip Crack like a cheap necklace.

"I think I'll send you to The Pools after all. When you return, if you survive long enough to get your memories back, you will know I have your mate. She will be broken by then. She will be mine."

A cruel grin spread across his face as he lifted me higher into the air. "But first, watch me destroy your precious sanctuary."

He raised his staff and drove the butt end at one of the walls. The impact of the blow was far more than it should have been. Gastrith was big, but he wasn't a seventy-foot giant. His staff, however, hit with the power of a C-4 shaped charge, sending crushed cars flying as if they were crumpled paper.

This was it. I'd had a good run, but my mouth had bitten off more than my body could chew. There was no fighting this demon. My best weapon barely scratched him, and he had a car exploding staff with the court jester sight option on top. He would crush me like a grape, and there was nothing I could do to stop him. My only regret was Alex. Why did she have to come? This would have been so much easier had I been alone. Well, maybe not easier ... but at least Alex wouldn't be hurt.

I willed her to open her eyes. She just laid there, motionless on the ground. Part of me hoped she was dead. At least Gastrith wouldn't be able to enslave her that way. We would suffer the Gnashing Fields together and come back out scarred, but whole again.

Gastrith raised his staff and prepared to drive it down again. His grip on my throat was unrelenting, and I began to lose consciousness. My eyes fluttered, and the world started to go black, then something else happened.

Not a strike from Gastrith's staff. Something deep and booming. I realized I was now on the ground, and I looked up, rubbing my throat with my hands. I gasped for air, struggling to pull in all I could, then I saw it ... or rather her. Mastema. She swooped in above Gastrith, holding a pair of ancient looking flintlock pistols in her hands. She fired at him again and again, the boom echoing so loudly I had to put my hands over my ears. Gastrith's chest, shoulder, and thigh opened up in a myriad of gruesome injuries. They looked more like outward explosions than bullet wounds, causing him to stagger back with every explosive blast.

As far as I knew, guns didn't work in Hell, so this pair of calamity creations must have been made specially for her.

Mastema didn't have her blindfold, and she darted around Gastrith like a falcon playing with its food. He swept his staff through the air in wild arcs, but it was no use. As if to punctuate her dominance, Mastema drew down on the head at the top of his staff and with a final blow detonated the little jester in a shower of smoke, flame, and splintered wood.

Gastrith screamed, and his hands went to his face as if she had torn his eyes right out of their sockets. As soon as he stopped fighting, Mastema holstered her weapons in a pair of belts strapped to her thighs, then went in for the kill.

The ferocity with which she tore at Gastrith reminded me of a raptor. She slashed and cut at his neck and torso with her claws. He went down hard on his back, and she stood there on his chest, peering around, looking as impassive as a cat. When Gastrith didn't move anymore, she took off, soaring away without glancing in our direction or acknowledging that we were even there. She just abandoned me to pick up the pieces alone.

CHAPTER FORTY-FIVE

"Hey, can we have another round over here?" Alex waved her hand and shot our Topside bartender a gleeful grin.

"Whoa, what has you in such a good mood? Remember what happened last time we had a few drinks up here? It wasn't pretty."

"We're celebrating. How often do we get to do that? And for doing good deeds."

"I know. I'm surprised you're not all itchy from the experience."

Alex backhanded me in the chest. "I'm not allergic to doing good deeds; it's just detrimental to my career, that's all. A point I've been rethinking quite a bit lately."

I started to ask what she meant by that when the bartender interrupted us with a matched pair of Jack and Cokes. He set them down on the table and swept up the empties.

"You two planning to pay for these this time, or are you going to find another patsy to foot the bill?" His voice grumbled with a distinct mix of admiration and disdain.

I held up a one-hundred-dollar bill followed by a grin.

"This one's all on us today."

The bartender took the cash without another word and headed back to the bar. I tried to act casual, but Alex had turned into a stone staring statue.

"Where did you get that?"

I shrugged. "Cash doesn't have much value in The Nine. You'd be surprised how easy it is to lay your hands on it, if you know who to talk to."

Alex shook her head. "Sometimes you amaze me. Usually it's because you've done something so stupid, but this ... this is pretty good."

I let out a laugh. "Easy on the compliments, or you're going to get itchy again. And the cash is nothing." I pulled a folded napkin out of my pocket and unwrapped it to reveal four white pills.

"What are those?" Her eyes narrowed in suspicion.

I sat back as if to say I couldn't believe she didn't know already.

"These are Excedrin hangover pills on steroids. Two of these, and you'll feel right as rain back in The Nine."

Alex eyed me with more than a little suspicion. "Yeah, right. What's in them?"

I folded the napkin and put the pills in my pocket for safe keeping. "I have no idea, but I'm pretty sure they would get us both arrested if we were caught with them up here. Either way, I swear they work. A friend was nice enough to give me a few, and I thought I'd share them with you."

Alex picked up her glass and smiled. "In that case, here's to doing good deeds."

We both took a drink and sat back in our chairs.

"How long do you think it will take to rebuild Hula Harry's?"

I shrugged. "He has lots of help. Zoe had half the Fresh-borns in The Nine working for him. I'll bet he'll be up and running in a few weeks. Plus, word's out that a couple of demon fighting Judas Agents like to frequent the place. I hear business is already beating down his door to hang out with the cool kids."

"Are you going to fess up on how you beat that guy?" Alex gave me a shove with her elbow. "I have a bet with Dan that says Gastrith tripped and fell on his own staff."

Alex had woken after the fight to see Gastrith limping away with his chest ripped out, and the only Woebegone left standing had been me. Too bad Mastema hadn't finished the job. Maybe it was against Hellion code. Maim, not murder, or something like that. Either way, I doubted we would be seeing Gastrith anytime in the near future. At least I hoped not. If I saw any clown again, it'd be too soon.

"Maybe he just got tired of punching my face."

Alex laughed at that.

"Doubtful. I mean who would get tired of that?"

That even made me laugh, but I settled down a little faster than she did.

"What's wrong with you?" Alex gave me poke. "This is supposed to be a celebration, remember? Why do you look so glum all of a sudden?"

"Just thinking of the trouble I've dragged you into lately. Simeon, Jake, Dan and his bar, Zoe."

Alex put a finger in my face and leaned in close at that last one. "I still owe you for leaving me at Dan's when you went after Zoe. I haven't forgotten about that. Partners don't leave each other behind."

I looked down at the table. "I know. The risk was so high, though. I didn't want you to get caught with the shield genera-tor, or worse, be linked to what had happened to the Wax Worx." I lowered my voice even though no one around would know what I was talking about. "Word is they're looking pretty hard for whoever's responsible for that one."

Alex reached up and grabbed my ear lobe and pulled it

toward her, making me wince and just about fall out of my chair.

"Get this straight." She spoke directly into my ear like a microphone. "If I want to take the risk, it is my choice, not yours. If you ever leave me like that again, I will tear off both your ears and feed them to my goldfish."

She let go, and I sat back up again, rubbing my ear. "All right, all right. No more partner ditching, but only if you promise to leave my ears out of it from now on."

"Fine, no pinching, twisting, pulling, or nibbling."

My eyes went up to her, and I stuttered like an idiot. "Wait...nib..."

Alex grinned in satisfaction and took a drink of her Jack and Coke. "Besides, that other stuff has me just as curious as you. I may not want to admit it, but I want to know what Simeon's up to as much as you do. Jake too for that matter. And Zoe is my friend as well. I want to know she's all right."

My eyebrows went up in astonishment.

"What? This whole train thing put a few things in perspective for me. Like maybe there are things more important than my comfy bed at the Agency."

"Okay, stop." I put my hand on Alex's head and felt for a fever. "Someone call an ambulance. My partner's been poisoned." I raised my voice and looked around the bar in a panic. "Someone poisoned my partner with a conscience."

Alex slapped my arm. "Shut up. All I'm saying is, maybe I've been riding you a little too hard. I could lighten up a little."

I smiled. "You've seen what kind of trouble I get into on my own? Don't you dare."

Alex laughed again, then we sat there just enjoying each other's presence for a moment.

"I'm glad you're all right," I said, finally breaking the silence between us. "I mean in that fight, I was worried you were gone. I'm glad you're okay."

Alex shouldered me and grinned. "Thanks. If it means anything, I'm glad you're not dead too."

I snorted out a laugh then sipped my drink. When I put it down, Alex had her eyes glued on something across the room. Her mouth was half open, and she had her palms pressed hard against the table.

I spun, looking for the trouble that had her so spooked, but all I saw were a few innocuous patrons, and a big screen television ... Then the scene changed, and I saw what had Alex so worked up.

Simeon Scott spoke to a reporter on the screen. He was, of course, in the hijacked body of Ryan Rokuda, now sole owner and president of MiRACL, The Micro-Robotic Advanced Cure Leaders company. There was no sound, but the caption under his name read: Unprecedented inoculation trials granted through legislature.

"Sir," I shouted at the bartender. "Can you turn that up for a moment?"

He grabbed a remote from behind the counter in time for us the hear the tail end of the report.

"... is a revolution in medical technology, and we want to be able to share it with everyone," Simeon was saying. "With the airborne inoculation program, our nanites can be transmitted from person to person everywhere, inoculating the world population without the need to go to a doctor or clinic. Our nanites can be shared on a bus, at a restaurant, to our families in our own homes. We have all but wiped out cancer and now diabetes. They have even cured me of autism. Given enough time and development, there is nothing our nanites cannot cure within the human body. They should be shared the way we have fluoride in our water or oxygen in the air. With the approval of the airborne inoculation program, we are one step closer to making that a reality. It's only a control group for now, of course, but soon everyone in the world will benefit from the medical miracles we manufacture."

The camera switched back to a visibly stunned interviewer.

"What about those who might not want to be inoculated? Shouldn't people have a choice?"

The camera changed back to Simeon again and closed in on his bright, smiling face.

"Of course. We will always have protocols in place to protect the rights of those who wish to remain ..."

Simeon stopped talking, and his face fell slack for a moment, then he began to look around as if he were lost. The reporter tried to follow his manic movements with her microphone, then when she couldn't, she pulled back to speak herself.

"Mr. Rokuda, are you all right?"

She thrust the handheld microphone at Simeon again, and he seemed to focus on the camera as if noticing it for the first time. He stepped into it, moving much too close, causing his face to get big and go out of focus.

"He's lying. Simeon is a liar." His voice was loud, and there were muffled sounds of a struggle as the cameraman tried to wrestle his lens free of desperate hands. "Please help me. I'm Ryan. Simeon has my glasses, and I can't see. I can't see, and I can't get out."

Want to find out what happens with Gabe, Alex and Ryan?
Read War Origin Now

THANKS FOR READING!

Did you love Artful Evil? Join the C.G. Harris Legion to stay up to date on upcoming books, receive book intel, useless trivia, special giveaways, plus you'll learn about Hula Harry and get his Drink of the Week. https://www.cgharris.net/legion-sign-up-page

Let other readers know what you thought of, Artful Evil, by Leaving a Review

Find out what Gabe and Alex are up to next. Read chapter one of *War Origin*, book 4 in The Judas Files.

Buy Book 4 Now:
WAR ORIGIN

WAR ORIGIN

Chapter 1

Working for The Judas Agency was like waking up every morning knowing you had to get a root canal—with no anesthesia. The job had to be done, but unless you're some kind of crazy, tooth sadist, you knew your day was really going to suck.

"What do you mean start a war?" I jogged to keep up with my partner, Alex. She wore her usual Topside attire: long boots, black trench coat, jeans, and a tee with strategic wear-holes to display the myriad of tattoos on her milky white skin. Her long hair, pulled back in a ponytail, read all business were it not for the Ty-D-Bol blue color. My style wasn't as edgy as Alex's. Brown and orange patchwork Gore-Tex and a buzzcut. Great for durability, but it wouldn't get me a red-carpet interview at the Emmys.

"I don't want to start a war in the middle of Los Angeles."

We had dropped into the city looking for an out of the way place to carry out our mission. When I say dropped in, I mean we used the Envisage Splice, a nausea inducing transport that allowed us to travel from The Nine—a cheery spin on Dante's euphemism for the deepest depths of Hell—to the land of sunshine and breathing. And right now, it was the breathing that was giving me trouble.

"Can we slow down?" I said between breaths. "I don't think qualifying for the L.A. Marathon is part of our mission."

"Sorry." Alex slowed from her power walking pace to that of a grocery store stroll. "I just want to beat the noonday lunch rush. Another hour and we would be waist deep in suits, construction workers, and bicycle couriers."

I took a moment to catch my breath. We were dead. It didn't seem fair that we should still get tired. Technically speaking, I shouldn't even have to breathe, but here I was, wheezing like the little train that could after a few blocks of smog wogging.

"You should get in better shape." Alex raised an eyebrow at me as I paced along beside her. "I'm not saying you need to be an Olympian, but this is ridiculous."

"I work out at least five-ish times a week." It was true. Ever since Alex had started training me in the fine arts of fist to face fighting, I had decided a little cardio wouldn't hurt. I had no idea why I sucked wind now.

"Well, next time you're on the treadmill, try turning it on. They work much better if you're not just standing on it."

I shot her a narrow-eyed glare. "Can we get back to the question at hand?" Alex rolled her eyes in obvious frustration.

"We're not starting a real war. Sabnack sent us on a mission to stir up discontent among the local street gangs, that's all. It's not like we're carpet bombing Hollywood Boulevard, so relax."

Sabnack was our department supervisor. Half man, half lion, all demon. He assigned us to our delightful missions to create havoc and mayhem on behalf of The Judas Agency.

"I never thought I would be relieved to hear the words 'gang war.'" I nodded.

"I'm so glad you feel better. Now can we get moving? We aren't in the best part of town." She sped up but kept a more reasonable pace than she had before.

Now it was my turn to scoff as I caught up with her. "They can't hurt us. What are you worried about?"

As long as we were Topside, any injury would heal instantly. At least anything caused by normal means. There were a few things that could harm a Niner, a Woebegone visiting from The Nine, but I was betting a typical bystander wouldn't have our brand of kryptonite on hand.

"I am less worried about us and more worried about them. What if some idiot shoots you in the face for talking too much? Which is a real possibility by the way. Should we lay waste to the whole town? Plus, how would you explain the fact that you came out of it looking as ugly as always."

"Ouch." I rubbed my face with my hand. "You think I talk too much?"

Alex rolled her eyes again and kept walking.

"So how many people are we talking about? I mean with the whole gang thing. I know it's not a full-scale war but..."

I trailed off as we rounded the corner of a high-rise building and wandered right into the middle of a huge crowd of people. I couldn't believe I had missed all the chatter and chanting. Maybe I did talk too much.

Alex and I backpedaled a few steps and slid off to the side, watching as they walked by. Many of them carried signs that read things like *Our Body, Our Right* and *Lockdown Government Poison*. They all wore surgical masks, bandanas, or face coverings of one kind or another and passed out flyers to anyone who would accept them.

I looked over at Alex. "This is not going to help our low profile."

One of the surgical mask bandits offered me a bright orange flyer, so I took it and read the bold title.

The headline said, "Stop MiRACL."

Alex read the blocked letters over my shoulder as well. The name made us both glance up and lock eyes. Earlier in the year we had a major run-in with the corporation, along with its new CEO and President, Ryan Rokuda.

To be accurate, it wasn't Ryan at all, but rather a fellow resident of The Nine named Simeon Scott. He had possessed Ryan and hijacked not only his body but also his company and had exploited his revolutionary medical breakthroughs ever since. Alex and I had seen Ryan push past Simeon's spirit for a moment and plead for help on national T.V., proving he was still a prisoner inside his body. We had been looking for a way to help him ever since. Easier said than done considering we had no idea how to extract the spirit of a Niner from a living human, and I was under strict orders from my boss, the one and only Judas Iscariot, to stay far away from Simeon/Ryan altogether.

The whole thing was insane, and now MiRACL had developed what they believed was the cure for all disease in our generation. A self-replicating nanite that not only adapted to a human's health needs, but it also spread through the air like a common cold, inoculating new people with nanites each time a carrier came into contact with the general population.

On one hand, it seemed like a modern miracle, pun intended, spreading like a micro autonomous superhero to cure disease on its own. On the other hand, MiRACL invaded peoples' bodies without their permission, and Americans in particular were not happy about it. Once released, it would only be a matter of time before the nanites reached every man, woman, and child on the planet, whether they wanted them or not. If there was one thing Americans would not stand for, it was someone taking away their right to choose.

"I heard about this," Alex said. "I didn't know they planned to demonstrate today, but they've been holding protests all over the country. Apparently, the U.K. had a Smallpox outbreak. No one can explain it since the disease has been wiped out for years. People up here think Ryan ... Simeon had something to do with it. They believe he weaponized the Smallpox in order to back them into a corner. I hear he's moved his whole base of operations to Europe, and they are planning to release his self-propagating nanites to fight the disease."

The protest grew in intensity as Alex spoke. They chanted, screamed, and began to march over the top of cars and bang on windows. The crowd was beginning to turn ugly. Invulnerable or not, I wasn't sure I wanted to be here when this thing turned from protest to angry mob. These people just needed a primer to set off the explosion.

"Hey." A female voice rose out of the crowd. I searched the sea of people and landed on a woman who marched straight toward us. I felt Alex tense next to me.

The stranger was at least as tall as me, if not taller. Athletic and assertive. She wore baggy jeans that were a little short, a dark shirt, and peacoat so black it seemed to swallow the sunlight. Her stark white spiked hair matched her eyebrows and eyelashes, a glaring contrast to her dark, accusing eyes.

"You two." She raised an arm and pointed a finger in our direction. "You work for them. You work for MiRACL. I saw you on television with Ryan Rokuda." She looked around at the crowd then yelled, "They're spying on us. Get them!"

Buy Book 4 Now:
WAR ORIGIN

Haven't read the other books in The Judas File series? Get them now:

The Judas Files Completed Series:
   Book 1-THE NINE
   Book 2-NEW DOMINION
   Book 3-ARTFUL EVIL
   Book 4 - WAR ORIGIN
   Book 5 - FINAL RUIN

FIND OUT JUDAS' TOPSIDE POWER
IN THIS FREE SHORT STORY

Download EXILED now

When Judas finds out one of his agents has gone rogue, he must go Topside to personally deal with him; even if that means wielding his own power and facing the past that haunts him.

Exiled, a short story in the world of The Judas Files, follows Judas on a Topside mission where he must face his own demons.

Download EXILED now (https://BookHip.com/JZLRATN)

NOW ON AUDIO!
AVAILABLE ON ALL AUDIOBOOK PLATFORMS

The Judas Files are also available on audio read by award-winning narrator, MacLeod Andrews.

LISTEN TO THE AUDIOBOOKS NOW

Here's what listeners are saying:

"The book are a perfect blend of gritty thriller, heartwarming hidden hero, and dry humor. The narrator Andrews does an amazing job of bringing the characters and story to life."

"Well worth the purchase! Fantastic stories by C.G. Harris, stellar narration by MacLeod Andrews."

"If you are a fan of the Dresden Files type of hero who is equal parts sassy, lovable, and punchable, then you will love Gabe. I was utterly enthralled by this envisioning of hell and the creatures who reside there. I had never imagined the underworld in this way, but it makes perfect sense. The side characters show growth and charm throughout the story, and left me wanting more. The audiobook narrator did a fantastic job with the voices and emotion throughout the story. I highly recommend this!"

NEW SERIES BY C.G. HARRIS
VIRAQUIN VOYAGE - A SPACE PIRATE ADVENTURE

Ben Roberts hears voices ... Alien voices.

Aliens, robots, and spaceships all rolled up into one hilarious, page-turning series.

Book 1-Hometown Space Pirate

Book 2-Stowaway Star Runner

SCI-FI SERIES BY C.G. HARRIS
THE RAX: A YA APOCALYPTIC ALIEN SCIENCE FICTION TRILOGY

When the earth becomes a base for alien drug lords, humanity's fate rests on the shoulders of a blind teen and his small band of rebels.

Book 1-OUT OF DARKNESS

Book 2-INTO THE LIGHT

Book 3-DANCE IN SHADOWS

ABOUT THE AUTHOR

C.G. Harris is an award winning science-fiction and fantasy author from Colorado who draws inspiration from favorites, Jim Butcher, Richard Kadrey and Brandon Sanderson. For nearly a decade, Harris has escaped the humdrum of the real world by creating fictional characters and made-up realities. When not writing, Harris spends time collecting the illusive arcade token, from the golden age when Dig Dug and Frogger were king. Harris knows the value of such a collection will only be seen in the confused faces of those family members left behind long after C.G. Harris is gone.

Do you have questions, comments or ideas for future plots? Contact C.G. at: CGharrisAuthor@gmail.com

Follow Me on:

Made in the USA
Middletown, DE
11 October 2023

40658825R00141